Clickfinger

THE HAGSTONE CHRONICLES
BOOK TWO

MAVIS GULLIVER

Mavis Gulliver

Published by Cinnamon Press,
Meirion House,
Tanygrisiau,
Blaenau Ffestiniog,
Gwynedd LL41 3SU
www.cinnamonpress.com

The right of Mavis Gulliver to be identified as author of this work
has been asserted by her in accordance with the Copyright, Designs
and Patent Act, 1988. © 2014 Mavis Gulliver.
ISBN 978-1-909077-73-7
British Library Cataloguing in Publication Data. A CIP record for
this book can be obtained from the British Library.
Designed and typeset in Palatino and Lucida by Cinnamon Press.
Cover design by Adam Craig based on a design by Christopher Hull
for 'Cry at Midnight' from original artwork 'Moonlight Horse' by
Destinyvispro © agency: Dreamstime.com
Cinnamon Press is represented by Inpress and by the Welsh Books
Council in Wales. Printed in Poland

Acknowledgements

Grateful thanks to Jan Fortune and everyone at Cinnamon
Press for having faith in *The Hagstone Chronicles* and for
publishing this book as a follow-on from *Cry at Midnight*.
Thanks to Christopher Hull and Adam Craig for another
great cover. Thanks to writer friends, Lorraine Mace and
Joan Lennon for support and suggestions, to my daughter
Caryl for proofreading, to my grandchildren for urging me
to keep writing, and to everyone who read *Cry at Midnight*,
especially eleven year old Amelia Neilson who wrote the
first review. Huge thanks to my husband Richard for
endless support and encouragement, for listening to
innumerable versions of the story and for sharing my joy in
writing. Finally, thanks to Gylen Castle on the Isle of
Kerrera, and McCaig's Tower, Oban for inspiring the story.

For my grandchildren
Cerys, Olive and Josef

Part One

Chapter 1

There was something strange in the air. Despite the warm sunshine Merryn shivered and rubbed the goose pimples that had formed on her bare arms.

'Wait,' she said as she grabbed her brother by the shoulder. 'There's something wrong. I don't know what it is, but... I think we should go back.'

'Back!' Hamish exclaimed. 'Whatever for? We're nearly there. You can do what you like, but I'm not going back, not for anything.'

He ran to a curve in the track and called out, his voice shrill with excitement. 'I can see the castle. Come on. Don't be a spoilsport. It looks amazing.'

The sun slipped behind a cloud and Merryn's shiver turned to a shudder. It ran down the length of her back and even though it stopped when the sun reappeared, she had an uneasy feeling that someone was watching her. She looked back the way they'd come, but all she could see was a grassy track through the bracken.

Hamish called again, his voice impatient. 'Hurry up. I'm not waiting.'

Merryn didn't move. Something had made her shiver. Something had made her shudder and she had to know what it was. She scanned the hillside again, but nothing moved. She cocked her head to listen, but the only sounds were the distant roar of the sea, the cry of a gull and the croak of a raven.

'Right,' Hamish shouted. 'This time I mean it. I'm going without you.'

Merryn stamped her foot. 'Sometimes I hate you, Hamish MacQueen. I'm supposed to look after you but you never listen and I'll be the one in trouble if anything goes wrong.'

Hamish didn't bother to answer. He ran on and disappeared behind an outcropping rock. Merryn turned away. She took a few steps back the way they'd come, but she still sensed danger and she couldn't leave her brother to face it alone. Feeling both annoyed and apprehensive she forced herself to chase after him. As the castle came into view her necklace of sea-beans and hag-stones gave a sudden jolt. It rattled against her collarbone, making her yell out in shock. That proved it – something was definitely wrong. She swayed dizzily and fell to her knees.

'Hamish,' she screamed. 'Don't leave me.'

Hamish ran back and bent over her. 'What's the matter? Have you hurt yourself?'

Merryn trembled and gasped for breath. She couldn't answer. Her mind was whirling. The necklace had hung, unmoving round her neck ever since they'd left Tiree. Now, it was reminding her of things she'd tried to forget. It was warning her of danger, but was it also asking for help? Surely she'd done enough in the fight against evil. She'd saved Kester Witchbane. She'd put an end to the witch of Tiree and the last thing she wanted was another terrifying challenge.

'Not again,' she groaned as she clutched the necklace. 'Please, not again.'

She scrunched up her eyes and wished with all her might that she didn't have The Gift. But even as she wished, she knew it was hopeless. She had The Gift and she was stuck with it. It had led her into danger. It had thrown Hamish into danger too. She'd begged Roane, the Selkie, to take it away. But he'd told her that

The Gift had arrived at her birth and that it would be with her until the day she died. It had seemed exciting at first, knowing that she wasn't like ordinary mortals. Knowing that she'd inherited The Gift from her great-great-great-great grandmother, that other Merryn MacQueen of long ago.

Now, as if to confirm that The Gift couldn't be denied, the necklace began to pulse. A tremor ran round her neck as the magic travelled along the plaited thread, passed through the knots, and swirled round the sea-beans and hag-stones.

'No,' she begged. 'Please stop. Leave me alone.'

The necklace ignored her plea. The pulsing grew in intensity. It made her cry out in pain. She took it in both hands and tried to pull it off, but it wouldn't move. The harder she pulled, the tighter it grew.

'All right,' she gasped, 'you win. Just stop and let me think.'

The necklace loosened, the pulsing slowed but it didn't stop. It was telling her not to go to the castle. It was telling her of magic – magic of a most malevolent kind.

'Stop it.' Hamish pulled at her arm. 'You're scaring me. Who are you talking to? What's wrong with you?'

Merryn struggled to hold back her tears. She stammered as she tried to put her thoughts and feelings into words. 'It's… it's not safe…the…the castle…we can't go…you… have to stop.'

'You're the one who has to stop,' Hamish protested. 'Stop fooling about. Stop talking to yourself. Stop pretending that something's hurting you. Come on, get up.'

Merryn choked on a sob. 'I'm…I'm not pretending. Honestly I'm not. It's awful. It's…it's happening all over again.'

His voice had been loud and angry. Now it cracked with anxiety. 'I don't know what you're talking about. What's happening again? Come on, you've got to tell me.'

'That's the trouble,' she wailed. 'I can't explain. I just know that we can't go to the castle.'

As if the necklace was satisfied with her words, the pulsing almost stopped. There was just a hint of what it had been. Hamish, on the other hand, was far from satisfied. He was furious. He jumped up and tried to pull her to her feet.

'Now you're talking rubbish,' he said. 'You're imagining things. It's just an old castle and I'm going inside. Come on, don't be a spoilsport. We can be there in a few minutes.'

Merryn pushed him away. She took a deep breath and forced herself to calm down. She looked at the castle through half-closed eyes. 'We can't. It isn't safe.'

'Don't be silly,' he said. 'They'd lock it if it was dangerous. Come on. We can pretend it's ours. It'll be fun. We can defend it against pirates and Vikings and aliens and…'

'Malevolent Witches,' Merryn whispered, 'except…'

'Except what?' Hamish demanded.

'Except…' Merryn swallowed the lump that had risen in her throat. 'Except I think they got there first.'

'Oh, for goodness sake!' Hamish exclaimed. 'There's no such thing as witches. Come on. You're wasting time.'

'Don't rush me,' she snapped. 'I need to think.'

10

Hamish muttered something incomprehensible. He kicked at a clump of rushes. 'One minute, then I'm going.'

For Merryn, their adventure on Tiree was as clear as if it had happened yesterday. For Hamish, it had faded just as Kester said it would. He'd forgotten everything and somehow she had to convince him that witches really did exist. The castle certainly looked impressive, perched near the top of the cliff with the sea and the hills of Mull beyond. She wanted to believe there was nothing sinister about it, but the necklace was telling her otherwise.

She squinted at the castle and gasped. It was as if two photographs had been printed onto one sheet of paper. The castle with its ancient walls was on top. But there was something underneath, something that rippled like the reflections in a rock pool when the tide floods in. Overcome with confusion, she shook her head.

'I don't know what it is, but it's more than a castle. There's another building mixed up with it. I can't see any windows or doors. It's like a fortress or a prison. It's magic, bad magic. I can feel it.'

Hamish laughed. 'You're crazy. It's a castle. That's all there is to it and I'm going inside.'

She grabbed his arm and clung to him with both hands. 'No. You've got to listen. You've got to let me explain. You don't unders…'

Her words tailed away as he wrenched himself free. Before she could stop him, he was running along the path, his arms outstretched like wings, his voice imitating the roar of an aeroplane.

Bewildered by a fear that wouldn't go away, she ran after him. She had to stop him before he went into the castle, but the track was confusing. It seemed to circle the rock on which the castle stood. Every time she glanced up there was a different view of the high walls. Every time she looked ahead there was no sign of Hamish. Where was the entrance? Had she missed it? Was her brother already inside?

Chapter 2

The ground began to rise steeply. The castle disappeared over the ridge and there was still no sign of Hamish. Out of breath and sobbing with anxiety she struggled up the castle mound. Suddenly the topmost turrets re-appeared and as she ran towards them the castle seemed to grow. It rose up, higher and higher, and beyond it there was nothing but sea and sky. Now she understood. The castle wasn't built on the top of the hill. It was set into the side of the cliff.

The necklace continued to thud against her collarbone, warning, warning, warning, but she couldn't stop now, for there, at last, was Hamish. Relief flooded through her. He hadn't gone inside! He was waiting for a crowd of people to come up the staircase from the castle entrance. Quickly she ran and caught him by the arm.

'Thank goodness I've stopped you,' she panted.

'You haven't stopped me,' he said. 'When those people have gone I'm going inside. Let go!'

Determinedly she clung onto him, her fingers tightening round his wrists.

'I mean it, Merryn. Let go or I'll kick you.'

Merryn hung on, but Hamish flew into action. He landed such a hefty kick on her shins that she yelped and let him go. Before she could grab him again he'd reached the steps.

'Come back,' she cried. 'It isn't safe.'

Her words turned to a gasp when she saw the creature that appeared in the doorway. It had the body of a cat, the face, ears and tail of a cat, but it was no ordinary cat. It was bigger than the biggest cat she'd ever seen. It spat and snarled as it sauntered onto the first step.

'Look out,' she shouted. 'There's a wild cat. It's coming to get you.'

'You can't fool me,' he called. 'You're just trying to scare me.'

'I'm not. It's true. Come back. Now.'

The cat advanced. It climbed onto the second step. It swished its tail and gave a high-pitched yowl.

'Listen to me,' she screamed. 'I'm not lying. It's like the horse. Remember, you couldn't see him at first.'

Hamish stopped and turned to look at her. His mouth fell open and he scratched his head as if he was trying to remember something.

'Kester, the horse,' she shouted. 'You must remember.'

'I thought that was a dream,' he stammered, 'but it's coming back to me. We saved him, didn't we?'

'Never mind that now. Come away before the cat gets any closer.'

Hamish looked round, his voice rising in panic. 'I can't see it. Where is it? Tell me what to do.'

'It's on the second step. Don't turn round. Just walk backwards. I'm at the top, waiting for you.'

The necklace throbbed even more strongly. Merryn winced at the pain, but she kept on talking. 'Keep going. You'll reach me in a minute.'

The cat crept slowly up the stairs, a growl rumbling in its throat, its tail lashing furiously. As Hamish reached the top step he stumbled back into Merryn's arms. A blur of fur and a flash of teeth hurtled towards them. Merryn tensed, expecting claws to rake through her skin, sharp teeth to sink into her throat. But the cat didn't reach her. Instead, there was a horrendous thud. It threw both her and Hamish off balance. They landed on their backs on the grass, gasping for breath, wondering what had happened.

Merryn struggled to sit up. The cat was barely a metre away. It was sitting on its haunches, its great head hanging down, its long barred tail lying still.

'It's all right,' she gasped. 'We're safe. We're back inside the bubble and it can't reach us. Look, it's stunned. It doesn't understand.'

Hamish hid his face behind Merryn's back. 'If it's magic I don't want to see it. We're going to be on Kerrera for ages and if we get mixed up in magic it'll spoil everything.'

Merryn ignored him. She grasped his arms and turned him round to face the cat.

'You can push me all you like,' he grumbled, 'but I couldn't see it before and I won't be able to see it now. I'm not even going to open my eyes. Anyway, I don't believe there is a cat. I bet you made the whole thing up to keep me away from the castle.'

Merryn sighed. 'Why would I do that? I want to explore the castle just as much as you. At least I did, until I felt the magic. Don't you remember? The necklace lets me see magical beings, and when I'm touching you, you can see them too. If you don't look at the cat you won't know where it is. You might walk straight into it. Open your eyes, Hamish. Now.'

Hesitantly, Hamish peered through his fingers. 'Crumbs,' he squealed. 'It's…it's a blooming panther,'

'Don't be silly,' said Merryn. 'Panthers are black. It's a magical cat and I bet it belongs to a witch. I told you there was bad magic about. It's inside the castle. I can

15

feel it. I can see it. Now that I'm holding you, you'll see it too. Go on, take a look and tell me what you see now.'

Hamish scanned the castle and nodded in agreement. 'You're right, there is something else, only it's blurry. I can't make sense of it, and what about the people who came out. The cat didn't bother them.'

'Well it's bothering us,' said Merryn. 'It's trying to keep us away. I don't know why and I'm not waiting to find out. Come on. The sooner we get away from here the better.'

'I'm not turning back now. I know the cat scared me,' he said, 'but I'm still going in. Anyway I bet it isn't after me at all. It's after you because of the necklace. You can go back if you want, but you can't make me.'

Merryn put her hands on her hips and frowned. 'Listen to me, Hamish MacQueen. Kester said you'd remember everything if another challenge came along. Well, you've started to remember. That means there is another challenge whether you like it or not. He also said that the experience you gained on Tiree would help you. So you'd better start to think about it. The bubble saved us from the witch, and just now it saved us from the cat. The bubble goes with the necklace. I'm wearing the necklace so the bubble stays with me. We don't know how far it stretches, and once you step outside it, there'll be nothing to stop the cat from eating you alive. You've got to stay close to me so you mustn't try to go to the castle.'

'But I…'

A sudden beeping put an end to their conversation.

'It's coming from the cat,' said Merryn. 'Look, there's a red light and it's flashing.'

'It must be on a collar,' said Hamish.

As he spoke, the cat leapt into the air. Its fur stood on end. It turned and twisted its head as if it was trying to get away from something. A howl of pain was followed by a sudden puff of smoke. When the last wisp had vanished, the cat had gone.

'That proves I'm right,' said Merryn. 'Someone sent the cat and now they've called it back. It's a witch. I know it is. I must warn The Benevolent Wizards. I need my crystal.'

She grabbed Hamish by the hand and pulled him along. 'Come on, there's no time to waste. If the cat tells the witch what happened, we'll be history.'

Hamish looked up at the castle. 'I don't know what to believe,' he muttered, 'but it was odd, the way the cat disappeared. I suppose I'd better come with you, but I'll be back. One of these days I'm going inside whether you like it or not.'

Chapter 3

Once the castle was out of sight, the necklace stopped pulsing. Were they safe – or would the evil power follow them? The sooner the Benevolent Wizards knew what she'd discovered, the safer she would feel. She hurried Hamish along, eager to contact Kester, furious with herself for packing the crystal along with her other belongings.

Hamish grumbled all the way. He scowled whenever she caught his eye. She understood how he felt. The thought of living on Kerrera until their parents found a new house had made them jump up and down with excitement. They'd expected an entire island to explore, now it seemed, the best part was out of bounds.

'You've timed that perfectly,' said Mum as they went inside. 'The removal men have gone and your things are upstairs. You'd better go and unpack.'

Merryn rushed to her room and frowned at the pile of cardboard cartons. Inside one of them was a carved wooden box, and inside that was the crystal that Kester, the young wizard, had given her. It was her only means of contact, the only way she could tell him that she'd discovered malevolent witchcraft. But which carton was it in?

She rummaged through carton after carton, tossing clothes onto the bed, piling books onto the windowsill, growing more and more frantic as the box failed to appear. The heap of clothes grew. The piles of books began to topple, and still she couldn't find it.

Hamish came to the door. 'It's all come back to me,' he said. 'The witch and Kester. He told you to keep the crystal with you always. You shouldn't have packed it.'

With growing impatience she frowned at him. 'I know, but look, I've found it.'

She opened the box and took out a twist of tissue paper. As she tore it open her heart skipped a beat.

'Something's wrong.' Her forehead knotted in a frown as she held the pink crystal up to the light. 'It's lost its sparkle. Something's happened to Kester. He might...' She choked on the thought and her voice petered away to a whisper, 'he might even be dead.'

'He can't be,' said Hamish. 'He couldn't die after we saved him. I bet he's so happy to be home that he's forgotten us.'

'He'd never do that.' She clasped the crystal in her hand. 'Kester,' she whispered. 'I need you. Please come.'

There was no response.

'At least say something,' she begged. 'Tell me you're all right.'

Hamish shrugged. 'I bet he never meant to come back. He just wanted rescuing, and now he's free he doesn't care about us.'

'That's not true.' Her voice rose indignantly. 'He does care. He'd come if he could.'

'But he said he'd send someone else if he couldn't come, and he hasn't done that either,' said Hamish. 'He's let us down and I think he's jolly mean.'

Hamish was filling her head with doubts. Could Kester really have forgotten? After the adventures they'd shared it didn't seem possible. She remembered the way he'd put the crystal in her hand and promised to come if she ever needed him.

'No,' she insisted. 'Something is blocking him, and I bet it's a witch in Gylen Castle.'

She placed the carved box on her lap. That was where the magic had started. That was where she'd found the necklace of sea-beans and hag-stones. If the crystal had lost its power, surely the box would help. Just like the first time on Tiree, her finger took on a life of its own. It reached out to touch the intricate carving. It followed the curves of the pattern that has no beginning and no end. But suddenly it stopped. She tried to complete the pattern, but her finger refused to move.

'I don't understand. Last time, a voice called my name. It told me what to do. Now there's nothing. Something awful must have happened.'

'I bet it's the battle between good and evil,' said Hamish. 'Perhaps it's all over. Maybe the witches have won and all the wizards are dead.'

Merryn glared at him. 'Don't say that and don't even think it.'

She held the box close to her ear. 'Come on,' she urged. 'There's a witch and we need you.'

Sighing with disappointment she lifted the lid and took out the sea-bean. 'I'll call Roane,' she said. 'I don't know if he can help, but it's our only chance. Come on, we'll go down to the sea.'

'Oh, no you don't,' said Mum as she appeared in the doorway. 'You're not going anywhere until you've put everything away. What were you thinking? You should have opened one box at a time.'

'That's what I told her,' said Hamish with a smug smile.

Merryn scowled. 'I know, but I was looking for something important, and I need to go out. Please, Mum, just for half an hour.'

'Definitely not. By the look of this mess you'll be tidying until bedtime. If you get everything unpacked tonight, you can have the rest of the weekend to explore. You had a walk this morning, now it's time to get the house in order.' She turned to Hamish. 'That means you too.'

'That's torn it,' he grumbled. 'It's your fault for being untidy. Now we're stumped.'

Merryn clambered over the empty cartons to look out of the window. She leaned out, assessing the drop to the grass below. Could she get out without Mum noticing?

'Oh! No,' said Hamish. 'Not the window. We got away with sneaking out of Aunt Aggie's, but we can't do it here. If Dad found out he'd ground us. We've got to wait for morning.'

Merryn refused to give up. Once again she held the pink crystal and tried to contact Kester. There was no response. For the second time, she ran her finger round the carving on the wooden box. As before, it stopped before she could complete the pattern.

She picked up the sea-bean, prised the two halves apart and took out the purple-tinged seashell. Perhaps Roane could speak to her, after all, the sea was only a short distance away. From the shell's coils came the scents of the sea, seaweed, fish and the tarry smell of ropes. Out came the roar of waves, the tumble of shingle and the singing of seals. But she was desperate for something else. When she opened it on Tiree there had been a voice. Roane, the selkie, had called her name.

Now, through the sea sounds, it came again, 'Merryn.'

Her heart lifted. 'Roane,' she cried. 'Thank goodness you've answered. We need....'

Suddenly the shell filled with a crackling noise. She winced and held it away from her ear. The crackling grew louder, until, as suddenly as it had started, it stopped. The scent of the sea vanished. The sounds of the sea stopped and Roane didn't call her name again.

'I don't know what to do,' she wailed. 'Something's desperately wrong. It must be a witch and I think she's more powerful than the witch on Tiree. She's blocking my messages. She's listening. She knows who I'm calling. She might even know where I am.'

Hamish shuddered. 'If you're right we're more than stumped. We're trapped. We can't fight her on our own. We don't stand a chance.'

Later that night Merryn tried again to call Kester and Roane. It was no use. The crystal had not regained its sparkle. No voice came from the box. The Selkie's shell was silent. She doubled over, clutching her tummy, trying to ease the pain of anxiety, but it wouldn't go away. Sleep was impossible. Kerrera! Of all the places her parents could have chosen, why had they picked an island inhabited by a witch? She had to find a way to warn the wizards. But what could she do? She'd tried everything.

Chapter 4

In the middle of the night, the necklace began to throb. Merryn propped herself up on one elbow and cocked her head to listen. The unfamiliar house was full of strange sounds. From downstairs came the hum of the fridge. Through the darkness came the creak of timber, and from the shore came the roll of waves.

'Merryn MacQueen. Look out of the window.'

Wide awake now, she sat up and listened. Was it a dream or had someone really called her name?

The call came again. 'Merryn MacQueen. Look out of the window.'

It was the voice from the carved box. She threw off the duvet and dashed to the window. Nothing but a half moon illuminated the path, the gate and the outline of fuchsia bushes beside the garden fence.

As her eyes grew accustomed to the gloom, she saw something moving in the far corner. She opened the window and peered out, and as she did so, a figure stepped onto the lawn and beckoned. Her heartbeat quickened. Was the witch trying to trick her? Or had her message finally got through?

The figure beckoned again, but the moon slipped behind a cloud and the garden plunged into darkness. There was nothing to see until the moon crept out of the cloud and showed her the person who had answered her call. It wasn't Kester. Disappointment flooded through her, but at least someone had come, and, like Kester he was wearing a tunic, a sporran and a pair of shoes with strange upturned curls.

'It's a wizard,' she breathed. 'It's definitely a wizard.'

With her trainers in her hand, she tip-toed down the stairs, pulled on her coat and slipped out of the door. The wizard came forward and clasped her hands. He began to speak, but Merryn was so desperate for news that she couldn't wait for her questions to be answered.

'Where's Kester? Is he all right? Why didn't he come? Who are you?'

The wizard drew her into the shadows. 'I am Kester's uncle,' he said. 'My name is Tobias Witchbane and I assure you that Kester is safe. He did not come because he did not receive your message. Following his misadventure on Tiree his channel of communication with you was severed. This is not only for his sake. The future of all Benevolent Wizards depends on it. Soon he will graduate and then he may speak to you. Until then you must forget him and deal with me. I intercepted your message and came to find out why you called so urgently.'

'Because there's a witch in Gylen Castle,' said Merryn. 'She sent a cat to scare us away. It tried to attack us, but I was wearing the necklace of sea-beans and hag stones. So that stopped it.'

'Ah,' Tobias nodded his head. 'I understand, but what do you know of the witch?'

Merryn faltered. 'Nothing. I haven't seen her. I just think she's there.'

Tobias scratched his head. 'Without a description, I cannot tell who she is. If we are to counteract her spells we need more information. Tell me about the cat. Many witches have such creatures, and some are distinctive. We may be able to identify her through her cat.'

'It was striped like a tabby cat,' said Merryn, 'only it was huge and it had black rings round its tail.'

'Was any of its fur white?'

'No. It was brown with black markings.'

'That description applies to many cats,' said Tobias. 'It is not enough. Please try to remember more.'

Merryn closed her eyes and conjured up a picture of the cat. 'It had yellow teeth, and its eyes were green. It had long hair and it must have had a collar because there was a red light flashing on its neck. There was a beeping sound too.'

'And there was a puff of smoke and it disappeared,' said Tobias.

'Exactly,' Merryn looked up in surprise. 'Does that mean you know the witch?'

He patted her shoulder and nodded. 'You did well to call us for you have located one of the most ambitious Malevolent Witches of all time. We have been seeking her for many years.'

He touched the necklace of sea-beans and hag stones. 'This will protect you against the cat, but if you go inside the castle it will not save you from this particular witch.'

Merryn gasped. 'But...but what if she comes out of the castle?'

'In case that happens we must increase your protection,' said Tobias. 'Let me see the crystal which Kester gave to you.'

'It's no use,' she said as she pulled it out of her pocket. 'The magic has gone. I think the witch has blocked it.'

'She will not block it when I have finished with it.'
He took it from her, placed it between his palms and blew on it gently.

When he opened his hands, Merryn's face broke into a smile. Her crystal was glowing even more brightly than before.

'As long as you obey me, this should foil the witch,' he said. 'But if you go against my instructions, I cannot guarantee your safety. Do you promise not to tackle the witch on your own?'

Merryn had no intention of going anywhere near the witch. 'Of course,' she said, 'but can I do anything to help?'

'Indeed you can, but first I have to tell you the things you must not do. Firstly, you must not try to contact Kester. I could not re-instate the crystal's power without re-opening the communication channel between you. However, if you use it for that purpose, the witch will intercept your messages and that will be dangerous for you both. Now put it in your pocket and do not venture out without it.'

Merryn had no choice but to do as she was told. More than anything she wanted to see Kester, but for both their sakes she promised not to contact him.

'Secondly,' Tobias continued, 'you must not go into the castle. In fact, after today, you must not set eyes on it until I give you leave.'

'But what will happen if I do? And what do you mean by 'after today'?'

'If you can see her magical fortress,' Tobias explained, 'she will be able to see you. The cat guards her hiding place. She relies on his eyes and ears to deter unwanted visitors. If she had seen you yesterday

26

she would have sought you out, and I would have been too late to save you. As it is we stand a chance. Come with me quickly for there is no time to lose.'

Merryn backed away. 'I can't,' she said. 'It's the middle of the night. What if Mum and Dad wake up? What about Hamish?'

'Hamish is a problem,' said Tobias. 'It will be difficult to keep him away from the castle, but you must do so at all costs. Some of the magic from your last adventure still clings to him, and the cat will detect it.'

'It already did,' she said. 'It was going to attack him.'

'Then he had a very lucky escape. If you had not been there I dread to think what would have happened. Now, do not worry about tonight. Hamish and your parents will sleep until you are back in your bed.'

Merryn gulped. 'But why must it be me? Can't someone else help?'

'My child,' he said. 'You have been chosen to help the fight against evil. Like your great-great-great-great grandmother you have been blessed with The Gift. On Tiree it enabled you to find the necklace and to see the witch. Through its power you contacted Kester, Roane and the Fairy Folk. It helped you to free Kester and to destroy the witch who held him captive. Here it has enabled you to see the cat and to detect another witch's presence. This means you are involved whether you like it or not. Now, you must come with me. You have no choice. There is work to be done and without you, our plan will fail.'

Chapter 5

'I didn't ask for The Gift,' Merryn muttered. 'It's spoiling everything. It leads me into danger and if Mum and Dad find out they'll go ballistic. Besides, I'm scared.'

'I understand,' said Tobias. 'But your role is vital. As far as I know, you are the only human who can help. Remember too, that you were victorious on Tiree. You proved your bravery, and this time you will not be alone. My bodily form will disappear but the crystal will allow you to know where I am.'

He smiled reassuringly. 'The task ahead cannot be accomplished by you and I alone. Others will join us and you will be aware of their presence. We will never be far away, and we will do all we can to ensure your safety.'

Merryn hesitated. 'But how can that be? I've only just told you about the witch. How do the others know? How can you have made your plans so quickly?'

'Anything is possible in the world of magic,' he said. 'I am in constant contact with my fellow wizards. They know everything that has passed between us. You see, as long as we are not bewitched, we share our thoughts without the need for words. We have made a plan and are agreed on the action to take. Now take my hand. We must go to the castle without delay.'

Merryn stumbled back in shock. She hadn't said she would help. Yet Tobias was speaking as if she'd already agreed. She still had terrible nightmares about the witch of Tiree. It had taken all her strength and all her determination to get the better of her. Now there wasn't just a witch, there was a vicious cat too.

Overwhelmed with uncertainty, she shook her head. 'I don't understand. You said I hadn't to go near the castle and now you're making me go. It doesn't make sense. I don't…'

Tobias didn't wait for her to finish speaking. 'If there was another way I would take it, but without you and The Gift we cannot proceed. All the Benevolent Wizards are relying on you. Our future is at stake, and that of Kester too.'

The moment she heard Kester's name, Merryn knew she had to agree. However dangerous the task, she would face it. She'd already risked her life to save him, and she would do so again. If she refused, all the ordeals she'd faced on Tiree would have been for nothing.

'All right,' she said. 'I'll come. Just tell me what I have to do and let's get it over with.'

Tobias led her away from the house. Although she felt the warmth of his hand, she no longer saw his solid shape. He was reduced to a silvery shadow, a misty shimmer edged in darkness. She clutched his hand even more tightly as similar figures fell in step beside them. Out of the night they came, wizards without number, a silent army marching towards the witch's hiding place.

Just before the castle came into view Tobias called a halt. He motioned to the wizards to come forward. Merryn watched as they linked arms and formed a tight circle around her. Their magical silvery glow soothed her a little, but even so, she clutched the necklace and wished and wished that everything would turn out right.

Tobias began to speak. 'We must remain here, out of sight of the witch and her castle, but in spirit and in thought we will be with you all the way. Now listen carefully, for the success of our mission depends on you. You must walk to the castle as if you intend to enter. When the cat appears, you must pretend to be afraid.'

'I don't need to pretend,' Merryn protested. 'I'm terrified.'

'There is no need for that,' said Tobias. 'You know that the cat cannot penetrate your bubble, but you must imagine that it can. When it emerges from the castle, let it see that it frightens you. It will prepare to attack, but do not wait for it to spring. If it hits the bubble too soon it will give up the chase and all will be lost. You must choose the right moment to run and the cat will follow. When you reach me you must slow down. That will allow the cat to pounce. It will hit the bubble and your part will be over. You must not stop. You must not look back. Above all, you must not witness what happens next. What you do not see, you cannot tell. Your safety may be reliant on that fact. So keep on running until you are back in your house.'

He nodded gravely and the wizards moved aside to let her leave. 'Now you must go.'

A wave of panic surged through Merryn's chest. It interfered with her breathing and made her gasp. 'But what if the cat doesn't come out?'

'There is no question of that,' said the wizard. 'The cat is programmed to detect and deter those who have

The Gift. That is why we need your help. That is why we cannot proceed without you.'

'But what if the witch comes out?'

Tobias paused. His face grew serious. 'As long as the cat drives you away, I do not think that will happen. It is a risk we have to take, but we will be ready for it.'

Merryn clenched her fists so tightly that her fingernails dug into her palms. Almost rigid with fear, she peered over the top of the slope. She drew in her breath in shocked surprise, for Gylen Castle had vanished. It was the other building, the magical fortress that stood out against the night sky. She hesitated, but Tobias urged her to continue.

'Hold the crystal in front of you,' he said. 'It will give you courage and light your way. Do not delay. Every second wasted is a second in the witch's favour.'

Although her feet seemed rooted to the ground, Merryn forced herself up the castle mound. She crossed the grass and walked towards the flight of steps. She stared up at the sheer walls of the witch's fortress. They towered above her, bare and forbidding, walls without windows, walls without doors.

Suddenly, the cat's snarl cut through the night air. Merryn looked round. She clutched her chest and swallowed. Where was he? Why couldn't she see him? She rubbed her eyes to see through the witch's magic fortress to the real castle. Gradually the cat came into focus, standing at the foot of the steps, staring at her with glassy green eyes.

It seemed wary, as if it remembered its previous experience with the bubble. It cowered down and made no attempt to come towards her. Could it

31

possibly be afraid? She took a tentative step towards it, but it didn't move. Tobias had not anticipated this. If it didn't chase her, the plan would fail. Somehow she had to make it believe she was afraid. She put a hand up to her mouth and made her fingernails shake against her teeth. The cat rose slowly to its feet, then, apparently unconvinced, it sat back on its haunches and washed its paws.

If it didn't start to chase her, the witch would come out to see what was happening. Fear, real fear flooded through her. Her teeth began to chatter. Her body shook uncontrollably. The cat stood up, arched its back, stretched and slowly climbed onto the first step. A low growl came from its huge throat. Merryn turned and ran. Some strange magic lent wings to her feet. She ran as she'd never run before and the cat bounded after her.

Chapter 6

As Merryn ran, she searched frantically for the wizards, but they remained out of sight. There wasn't even a hint of their silvery shadows. On and on she ran, her breath coming in ragged gasps. The cat pounded after her. It was getting closer. It was gaining on her. If it pounced before she reached the wizards all would be lost.

With a last huge effort she neared the foot of the mound, and in that moment the cat leapt. As it hit the skin of the bubble she felt herself falling, tumbling over and over, her head thudding against the ground, the breath being forced from her body. She lay, gasping, unable to remember what she had to do.

Tobias grasped her and hauled her to her feet. 'Go,' he urged. 'Go home and do not look back.'

'But...but then what?'

'Go,' he ordered. 'You have played your part. The rest is up to us.'

Merryn flinched at the harshness of his words. After the danger she'd faced, after obeying all his instructions, Tobias didn't even thank her. She tried to do as she was told, but all her energy was spent.

As she hesitated, a different wizard took her by the shoulder. His voice was rough and insistent. 'Do as Tobias says or we may yet lose. Go, Merryn, go home. Make haste and whatever you do, do not look back.'

Still out of breath, still shaken by her fall, she stumbled away from the wizards.

'Hurry,' the wizard called after her. 'The witch will take advantage of every moment's delay.'

Somehow, Merryn forced herself to run. The magic that had spurred her on had faded. In a matter of moments a stitch forced her to stop. She bent double, waiting for the pain to subside as she tried to imagine what lay behind her. It would be so easy to peep over her shoulder to see what was happening, but the wizard's words echoed in her head. 'Whatever you do, do not look back'. She forced herself to look straight ahead, knowing that what she didn't see, she couldn't tell.

On she went, walking a few steps, jogging a few steps. Gradually she began to breathe more easily. The cat was left behind, but so were the wizards. She was on her own. There was no-one to protect her, and nothing but the necklace, the bubble and the crystal to save her from the witch.

Clouds thickened round the moon. The island darkness crowded in. The crystal gave enough light to guide her along the track, but what if it guided the witch too? What if she came out of her fortress? What if she was already close behind? Fear made her heart pound, but it also spurred her on. For the last few hundred metres she ran as fast as she could go.

Relief came as she passed through the gate into the garden. The house, just as she had left it, was in darkness. Carefully, she opened the door and closed it behind her. Inside at last, she paused and listened. Tobias had promised that Hamish and her parents would sleep until she was safely in bed, but she took no chances. She took off her trainers and tiptoed upstairs to her bedroom. She stepped inside, closed the door and listened. Thankfully, no-one had stirred.

She climbed into bed and snuggled down beneath her duvet. Her crystal shone with a bright pink glow. It proved that she'd been with Tobias, that she'd been helping the Benevolent Wizards. If she told Hamish he wouldn't believe her. He'd say it was a nightmare. Well it wasn't. It wasn't even a dream. She'd helped the wizards and now it was their job to vanquish the witch of Gylen Castle.

Despite the ordeal of the last few hours she smiled to herself. The crystal had not only regained its magic, it was even more powerful than before. If she needed Kester she could call him. A sudden frown wiped the smile from her face as she reminded herself that contact was forbidden. The temptation to call him almost overwhelmed her. But she'd made a promise, and she had to keep her word.

Restlessly she tossed about, her head filled with thoughts of wizards. What had they done to the cat? And why wasn't she allowed to see? Although she didn't want a confrontation with the witch, she felt she had a right to know what was happening. The wizards had needed her. They couldn't have managed without her. She'd done everything they asked, and now they'd sent her away.

Feeling thoroughly disgruntled she turned over and thumped her pillow. 'It's not fair,' she muttered, and with that thought foremost in her mind, she drifted into sleep.

For Merryn, morning arrived too soon. Still tired from her night's adventure, she groaned when Hamish barged into her room at an even earlier time than usual.

'Come on,' he said as he snatched the duvet. 'We have to contact Roane.'

Merryn snatched the duvet back. She pulled it over her head and clung to it. 'I thought you didn't want to be involved,' she said, 'and in any case, you're too late. I've done what had to be done. Go away. I've been out all night and I want to sleep.'

'I don't believe you.' Hamish leapt onto the bed and pummelled her 'You haven't been anywhere. You've been dreaming again.'

'I haven't.' She poked her head out of the bedclothes. 'I'm telling the truth.'

He sat back on his heels at the bottom of her bed. 'If you really have been out, if you left me at home while you had all the fun I'll never speak to you again.'

'Fun! Believe me, it wasn't fun,' Merryn retorted, 'and it's no good being mad at me. I did as I was told. Kester's uncle came for me. He made me coax the cat out of the castle. It chased me and it hit the bubble, but I don't know what happened next because I was sent home. He said we have to leave everything to the wizards and we mustn't set eyes on the castle until he tells us that it's safe.'

'It's not fair,' Hamish protested. 'It's bad enough when you do things without me, but the castle was the one thing I wanted to explore.'

'I know. It was the same for me,' said Merryn,' but you must promise. Tobias said that some of the magic from Tiree still clings to you and that's why the cat was stalking you. He said that the witch will detect it too. So I mustn't let you go anywhere near.'

Hamish seemed to consider for a moment, then he grinned. 'Nice try, Merryn, but I think you made it all up. You did it to stop me from going to the castle, but it won't work. I don't believe a word of it.'

Merryn slipped her hand under her pillow. Slowly, she uncurled her fingers. The crystal shone as bright as any star. Its pink light cast a rosy glow over everything in the room.

Hamish's jaw dropped. For once he was lost for words.

'There you are,' she said. 'There's proof. Tobias mended it. Now you'll have to believe me, and you'd better do as you're told and stay away from the castle.'

Part Two

Chapter 7

The supermarket trolley crossed the car park, weaving in and out of parked cars, dodging between groups of people, avoiding oncoming traffic. Emily clung to the handle and laughed delightedly. This was fun. But the fun didn't last because the speed increased, and her laughter turned to panic when she realised that she couldn't let go.

'Look out,' she shouted as she narrowly missed a mother with a pushchair. 'Look out,' she yelled as she swerved round an old lady with a walking stick.

People stopped and stared. They leapt out of her way. Cars hooted their horns. Children laughed. Still the trolley ran on, making her legs go faster than they'd ever gone before.

'Stop that crazy kid,' someone shouted, 'or there'll be an accident.'

Emily tried to stop, but the runaway trolley dragged her along.

'Help,' she screamed, 'my hands are stuck.'

No one came to her aid and it wasn't until the trolley smashed into the others in the shelter that her hands fell free. People crowded round her, all shouting at once. A woman called her a hooligan and a man caught her by the shoulder and shook her.

'You little fool,' he barked. 'You're lucky no-one was hurt. What on earth were you thinking?'

Emily had been too scared to think. She didn't have a reason. She didn't have an excuse. There was no point in trying to explain because no-one would believe in a trolley that moved by itself – a trolley that stuck to her fingers like superglue. She hung her head and refused to answer. People drifted away, muttering about bad-mannered kids. Red-faced and close to tears, all she wanted was to find her mum. But Mum was in the supermarket and she couldn't face the people who'd seen her careering across the car park. Besides, she was out of breath and needed time to stop her heart from pounding.

'There she is, that's the girl,' shouted the old lady with the walking stick. 'I'd give her a good hiding if she was mine. That's what she needs, stupid girl.'

Emily didn't wait to hear more. She couldn't have waited, even if she'd wanted to, for just then, something spun her round and made her run. She tried to stop, but it wasn't until she arrived at a strange car that her legs stopped pounding. She peered through the dirty windscreen, and there inside was an old woman wearing Great-gran's cardigan.

She blinked, rubbed her eyes and looked again. The cardigan was hers. It was all she had left of Great-gran. Bursting with indignation she tapped the glass. 'That's mine,' she shouted. 'You shouldn't be wearing it.'

As the woman turned and smiled, Emily's mouth fell open. The face was Great-gran's face, and the smile was Great-gran's smile.

'Great-gran,' she breathed. But it couldn't be because she knew that Great-gran was dead.

'Come on Em,' said the woman in Great-gran's voice. 'Let's have an adventure.'

Emily blinked and stared and all her doubts disappeared.

'Great-gran,' she yelled as she leapt into the car and flung her arms round the woman's neck. 'You won't believe how much I've missed you.'

The woman didn't answer. She didn't even hug Emily. She pushed her into the passenger seat and switched on the engine.

'Hang on,' said Emily. 'We can't go without Mum.'

She turned to get out of the car, but the door slammed and the seatbelt snaked across her chest and fastened itself.

'No!' she shouted. 'What are you doing? Where are we going?'

Her words were drowned by the revving of the engine as the car accelerated towards the barrier.

'Stop!' she yelled. 'You're going too fast! We'll crash!'

She clutched the sides of her seat as the engine's roar grew to a high-pitched whine. Her body tensed and she screwed her eyes up tight as she waited for the crash. It never came. Instead, the car rose and skimmed over the barrier in a cloud of thick, grey smoke.

The woman laughed a hideous, cackling laugh. It sent a shiver, like a trickle of icy water, down between Emily's shoulder blades. She opened her mouth to yell for help, but no sound came out. She tried to grab the woman's arm, but she couldn't move a muscle.

Mum, Mum! That one word screamed over and over inside her head. But there was nothing Mum could do. She'd be rushing round the supermarket, panicking because she couldn't find Emily anywhere. Only Mum didn't usually panic. Emily could almost hear her saying what she always said when there was a problem. Calm down. Think positive thoughts and it'll come right in the end. But Mum didn't know she was in a flying car with a mad old woman, and Emily couldn't think of anything to be positive about.

How could she stay calm when she'd been kidnapped? How could she be positive when the woman next to her looked exactly like her dead Great-gran? Anger flared through her fear. Whatever the woman did, wherever the woman took her, she'd get away and go back to her mum.

But what if she couldn't? What if she never saw her mum again? A sob caught in her throat. Fear swamped her anger. Her breathing grew faster and shakier. If only she could move. If only she could speak. But all she could do was stare into the thick grey cloud, her heart pounding and the ache in her chest getting harder and harder to bear.

The car jolted, swerved and tilted. Then it landed, bounced along the ground and skidded to a halt. Whatever had held her silent and immobile let her go. All the terror that had been building up inside her exploded in an ear-splitting scream.

'Stop that awful racket,' snapped the woman. 'There's no-one to hear you. So you might as well save your breath.'

Hearing the harsh words in Great-gran's voice was more than Emily could bear. She covered up her ears to shut out the sound. The seatbelt undid itself. The car door swung open and the woman pushed her out. Wet grass soaked into her clothes and all around her a thin mist swirled like grey ribbons in the wind. Stone walls rose above her. She looked round frantically. There must be somewhere to hide. But before she could pick herself up, the woman grabbed her arm and pulled her down a flight of steps, through a doorway into a stone-flagged passage. A glimmer of daylight shone at the far end. Emily wrenched her arm from the woman's grasp and ran through an archway into the misty air. She got one leg over the iron railing that barred her way before the woman pulled her back.

'You little fool,' she said. 'There's no way out, and definitely not that way. Just look where you were going.'

Emily looked down through gaps in the mist, past cliffs dripping with water and hung with ivy, down to where waves were crashing far below. If the woman hadn't stopped her, she would have slipped over the edge – falling, screaming, tumbling onto the jagged rocks. She clutched the railing and hung on as if she'd never let go, but the woman grabbed her hands and prised them free.

'Let me go,' shouted Emily as the woman pushed her up a stone staircase. 'I want to go home.'

'No chance,' said the woman. 'Search as much as you like, but you'll never find a way out.'

Emily ran up the steps, panic making her dash from wall to wall. There had to be a hidden door or a secret passage, but the stonework looked solid. She hurried from window to window, but all she could see were cliffs, a stony beach and the sea. And all of them were far, far below her. Even if she could squeeze through one of the windows she would need a very long rope, and even if she had a rope, she couldn't see a safe landing place. It was true. There was no way out. She leaned against the damp wall and sobbed.

'Pull yourself together,' said the woman. 'I can't stand tears. Cheer up. It's not a bad place to live. You'll soon get used to it.'

Chapter 8

The woman was definitely mad. No one could live in a ruined castle on a cliff top above the sea. Emily's tears fell faster. 'I want my mum,' she sobbed.

'Forget your mum,' said the woman. 'This is your home now.'

Home! How could this be home? Home was with Mum. Emily's knees buckled. She slid onto the stone floor, her nose running, her sobs growing louder.

'Stop this minute or I'll give you something to cry about,' yelled the woman.

She caught Emily by the shoulder, yanked her to her feet and prodded her with a bony finger. Emily took a few unsteady steps backwards but the woman followed and prodded again.

'I need you. As soon as I found the cardigan I knew you'd be useful, but I had to check. I spent a week watching you and I won't let you disappoint me.'

Emily couldn't bear to see Great-gran's face filled with so much anger. As for the woman watching her for a week, surely that had to be a lie. But the woman hadn't finished. She prodded Emily again.

'I saw you dancing in a concert. I heard you chatting to your friend Sarah. I followed you to school. I saw you come first in a spelling test. I watched you at home, washing up, watering a pink geranium. I saw you helping your mum to make a fancy dress. Then I saw the cardigan and that's what clinched it.'

It seemed impossible, but everything the woman described had really happened. Emily stuffed her fingers in her mouth to quell the sobbing. She wanted to deny it all. She wanted to call the woman a liar, but it was true. She wasn't just a kidnapper, she was a spy, a stalker and a thief. Emily went cold all over as she thought of the woman coming into her bedroom, opening her wardrobe and stealing Great-gran's cardigan.

The woman pulled her to her feet, grabbed her by the chin and tilted her face so that she could look into her eyes. 'I will not be thwarted,' she said. 'You talk to your mum and your friends so you can talk to me. I need someone who can sew, but I don't want a girl who spends half her time sobbing and the other half terrified out of her wits. If you don't want to end up like the rest of them you'd better start talking. Now what do you have to say?'

Emily stuttered. 'I.... I don't know.'

'You can do better than that. Tell me what you think of your new home.'

Emily's mouth opened and closed. She couldn't win. If she refused to answer she'd be in trouble and if she told the truth she'd be in trouble.

'I... it's not like a home. It's not... very... comfortable.' Her voice tailed away to a whisper.

'Speak up.' the woman insisted. 'Tell me what you really think.'

Emily stared at the woman who looked like Great-gran. If she'd behaved like Great-gran everything would have been fine. She could have talked to her all day. But what could she say to this horrible imposter? What dare she say?

The woman tapped her foot impatiently. She reached out to grab Emily's chin again, but Emily dodged aside. Her voice shook as something forced her to say what she really thought.

'It's horrible. No one can live here. There's no glass in the windows. There's nothing to cook on. There's nowhere to sleep.'

The woman pointed to the huge, stone fireplace. 'You'll cook on the fire and you'll sleep on the floor. What more can you want?'

Emily shook her head despairingly. 'You can't be serious. It's cold and damp. There's no furniture. There isn't a bath. There isn't even a tap for washing hands.'

'Huh! Who needs clean hands? Who needs a bath? And speak up, I can barely hear you.'

Emily swallowed and cleared her throat. Her voice came out in a squeak. 'I like baths and besides, there isn't even a toilet. We can't live without a toilet.'

'Don't tell me what we can't do.' said the woman. She pushed Emily towards a hole in the floor of a little recess in the wall. 'That's the toilet. The people who built the castle used it. It was good enough for them so it's good enough for you. All the poo drops onto the beach and the tide comes in twice a day to flush it away. Clever isn't it?'

Emily stared through the hole to the ground far below. Couldn't the woman see that it was dangerous? It might be all right for her but Emily knew she was skinny enough to fall right through. She backed away, shuddering.

'You'll manage,' said the woman. 'As long as you're careful.'

A cold breeze ruffled Emily's hair. The mist drifted away and a pair of ravens flew from the top of the wall. Up they went, filling the air with harsh calls. Emily stared at the open sky. When it rained, water would run down the stairs. And when there were gales, the wind would howl round the crow-stepped gables and wuther in the chimney.

'Let me go home,' she begged. 'No-one can live here. There isn't even a roof.'

She stood in the middle of the room and went over everything the woman had said. She thought about the journey in the flying car and the impossibility of Great-gran coming back to life. Even though the woman was the image of Great-gran she was definitely someone else.

'It's a nightmare,' she moaned. 'That's what it is. It's a beastly nightmare and in a minute I'll wake up. Nothing in real life could be as bad as this.'

'I fooled you.' The woman hooted with laughter. She kicked up her heels and her shoes clattered on the flagstones as she danced round Emily. 'I fooled you,' she chanted. 'I fooled you.'

Emily clamped her hands over her ears and turned away. But no matter which way she faced, the woman was always in front of her.

'Stand still, you stupid girl,' she said as she pushed Emily against the wall. 'It was a joke. I thought you liked jokes. You laughed at jokes with your friends.'

Emily lost her temper. 'It wasn't a joke,' she shouted. 'It was a mean, nasty trick. But then you're good at mean, nasty tricks. Kidnapping me was a mean...'

The woman cut her off with a sound that was somewhere between a snarl and a bark. She pointed a finger at Emily then hastily pulled it back and tucked it under her arm.

'Wretched girl,' she said. 'Why can't you do as you're told?'

49

'Because I don't want to,' Emily shouted. 'I don't want anything to do with you. I want to go home.'

'And I told you to forget about home. You're here to stay. You're here to work, and that's what you're going to do.'

Emily took a step forward. She shook with anger. She clenched her fists into tight little balls. 'You made me talk. You made me say the things I was thinking. I wasn't going to say them because I knew you'd be angry. You asked what I thought about this dump of a castle and you made me tell you. I knew you wouldn't like it but that's your fault not mine. Besides, I'm a child. I go to school. Children don't go to work so I'm not going to work and you can't make me.

'Huh! I can make you do anything I want,' said the woman. 'Just you watch me.' She turned her palm towards Emily's face. 'Stun-Dumb,' she said and she began to laugh.

Emily felt her body stiffening. In a matter of seconds she was as still and silent as a statue.

The woman nudged her. 'Stay there until you've cooled your temper,' she said. 'That'll teach you who's in charge. When I come back, if I come back, you'd better mend your manners. I want you to talk but you'd better be careful what you say. Do I make myself clear? '

With a grin and a wave she turned towards the stairs and was gone.

Chapter 9

Leaving Emily alone, the woman stamped down the stairs. 'Bat's blood,' she cursed, 'snake's skin and toad's innards. What in the name of witchcraft do I do now?'

She sat down on the bottom step, mumbling to herself and wondered how to deal with a girl who didn't seem afraid to answer back.

'Drat the girl. She's right to a point. I can make her talk but I can't make her say what I want her to say. I could if I made a different spell, but I haven't time. Besides, I need to know what she's really thinking. I could bewitch her to make her work, but that's too risky. If I use magic to sew my costume, those other crafty witches can use magic to pull it apart. They'll unpick every stitch when I'm in the middle of my act and then I'll be ruined. No. I can't use magic to make her work. She has to sew of her own free will.'

With a disgruntled sigh she thought of the children she'd captured over the years. None of them had answered back. And now, the one she needed most had the nerve to challenge her. If the girl had been anyone else she would have put an end to her in no time. The thought made her finger twitch. It twitched so much that it ached. She blew on it and rubbed it to take the pain away, but it didn't respond. It was itching to sort Emily out.

'Get this,' she said as she held it in front of her nose. 'I'm in charge and don't you forget it. There will be no clicking at Emily, or all my plans will fail.'

She got up, wandered to the doorway and wondered if the spell she'd used would have the desired effect. If it didn't, she would have to try something else. She muttered her way through all the possible spells, counting them off on her fingers, and discarding them one by one. She knew that most of them were risky, that the tiniest mistake could make Emily disappear forever. Whichever spell she chose, she would have to perform it with the utmost care.

A sudden ray of sun cut through the clouds, dazzling her eyes and making her blink. She clapped her hands delightedly. 'That's the answer! Weather! Standing up there in the sunshine won't bother her at all, but I know what will.'

She stepped outside, threw up her arms and ordered a storm. The wind arrived in a gust from the frozen north. It sent black clouds scudding past the castle walls and out to sea. At the first deafening clap of thunder she started to laugh. She laughed even louder at the crackling forks of lightning. But when the first huge drops of rain began to fall, she rushed to the vaulted cellar where the worst of the weather couldn't reach her.

'Ten minutes,' she said as she looked at her watch. 'That should make her think twice about arguing, and if she still hasn't learned her lesson, I'll give her another ten.'

She crouched under the low ceiling and wondered what to do if Emily still refused to co-operate. The Stun-Dumb Spell was safe enough. It would stop the girl from answering back, and it would stop her from doing anything stupid. As for refusing to obey orders, the Robot Spell that she'd used in the car-park would show her that she had no choice. Surely, if she used them both, the girl would realise that it was sensible to do as she was told. When that happened, there would be no need to control her with magic, and the real work could begin. But what if she still refused?

'I bet her great-gran knew how to deal with her,' she said. 'I bet she had some good punishments. She probably locked her in the coal cellar, or sent her to bed without any supper. Or better still, she fed her on dry bread and water for weeks on end. Whatever it was, her cardigan can show me.'

She closed her eyes, ran her hands up and down the sleeves, and concentrated on the secrets that were locked inside the stitches. The first thing she felt was the love that Great-gran and Emily had shared. 'Love,' she said with a sniff. 'Sentimental twaddle! Love has nothing to do with anything.'

But the cardigan seemed to think otherwise. It showed Great-gran hugging Emily, playing with her, telling her stories, comforting her when she was sad, helping her with homework and encouraging her when things were difficult. It was full of smiles and cuddles, kind words and gentleness. And although the woman searched every stitch, she couldn't find a cross word or a mean thought anywhere.

'So that's how she did it. Well. It's not my way. I'm not going to be soft and let her do as she pleases. Oh no! I've never said a kind word to anyone and I'm not going to start now.'

She buried her head in her hands and groaned. Maybe, just maybe, she'd have to be less hard on the girl. If nothing else worked it might be the only option, but the very idea of being nice to anyone made her want to vomit. She didn't think she could do it, but with her whole future at stake she might have to try. With that unpleasant thought in mind, she frowned and checked the time. Ten minutes had stretched to seventeen. Reluctantly she got to her feet and battled against the rain that howled in gusts down the passageway. From the doorway she shook her fist at the sky and commanded the storm to stop.

The clouds disappeared in an instant. The wind slowed to a gentle breeze and the rain stopped falling, but the stairs had turned into a raging waterfall. Long before she reached the top her shoes were squelching. But when she saw Emily standing ankle deep in water, hair like mouse tails, raindrops hanging from her nose, her ears and the knuckles of her clenched fists, her spirits rose.

'Drowned rat – or what?' She chortled as she walked round her. 'This is the funniest thing I've seen in years. If this doesn't wipe the defiant look off your face I won't just eat my hat, I'll eat my broomstick as well.'

She poked Emily in the ribs and reminded her of all the things she'd said before. With every sentence she uttered she poked Emily again, and when all the poking was over she waved her hand and broke the spell. She stepped back and watched through narrowed eyes. The girl began to shiver. She crossed her arms and tucked her hands under her armpits. Her teeth chattered and her breath came out in shaky little puffs.

'Well.' The woman gave a satisfied smile. 'What have you to say for yourself now?'

'Nothing,' Emily whispered.

'So you've seen sense at last. I thought that would do the trick. Now, are you sure you've nothing else to say?'

She raised her eyebrows and watched Emily expectantly. But the girl just shook her head and went on shivering.

'Good, now you're ready to co-operate I'll show you where you're really going to live.'

Chapter 10

The woman dragged Emily down the stairs, pulled her along the passageway and out into the fresh air. Even though the sun was peeping through the clouds, a chill wind made Emily shiver more than ever. But she was outside the castle and that was all that mattered. She forgot her dripping clothes and chattering teeth. The woman had lied. Of course there was a way out. It was the way they'd come in. She looked round, trying to get her bearings. On this side of the castle there were no cliffs and there was no sea. She looked round for signs of life, but there was nothing – not a house, not a fence, not even a sheep or a cow.

Her heart sank at the emptiness. Something must lie beyond, and when she escaped she would find out what it was. She would run and she wouldn't stop until she found someone to help her. A quick glance at the castle showed that there were windows overlooking the hillside, windows that the woman had somehow managed to block on the inside. If she could find them, she might be able to climb out and land on the grass.

The woman yanked her hand. 'Pay attention,' she snapped. 'If you don't want to live in the ruin you must do as I say. Are you ready?'

Emily tried to snatch her hand away. Of course she wasn't ready. She'd seen a way to escape and that was all she could think about. The spell that had frozen her was almost forgotten, but her tone of voice had changed. 'Please,' she pleaded. 'I'm not ready to do anything with you. I want to go home.'

The woman tightened her grip. 'I told you, this is home now. Pay attention and count with me.'

Without pausing for breath the woman began to count. Emily, unable to stop herself, counted too. On the count of seven, the woman leapt over the threshold and dragged Emily with her. The stone rooms disappeared and Emily found herself in the untidiest room she'd ever seen.

Her hand flew up to her nose to block out the stale smell, and she stared at the mess in disbelief. Armchairs were covered in tattered blankets, the floor and table were littered with books and papers. The only cheerful thing was a brightly burning fire. But it was the shelves that made her really stare. They filled the space between floor and ceiling and they were loaded with strange objects – stuffed animals, skulls, horns, crystal balls and spiky plants in pots. Among the stacks of books were jars and bottles in dozens of different shapes and sizes. They were filled with coloured liquids that glinted and sparkled in the flickering firelight. But something was missing.

Her voice rose in panic. 'Where are the windows? Where's the door?'

'Who needs windows?' laughed the woman. 'Who needs a door? We're not going anywhere.'

'I can't stay here,' Emily dashed to where they'd entered the room. She pushed and pulled the shelves so hard that bottles began to rattle and a sheep's skull fell to the floor.

'Stop it!' The woman raised her palm as she'd done before, but Emily ran to the fireside and dropped into one of the armchairs.

The woman gave a satisfied nod. 'Good,' she said. 'I see you've learned your lesson.'

Emily frowned. The only thing she'd learned was that she would have to be careful. Somehow she would escape, and if her first plan failed she would try another. She would go on trying until she got back home. As the woman turned away to stir something on the stove Emily's eyes filled with tears. It was hard enough losing Great-gran without having this mad old woman looking exactly like her. If she'd been wearing something else it wouldn't have been quite so bad. But the cardigan had been made for Great-gran, and no-one else had the right to wear it.

She closed her eyes and curled up in the chair. If she was quiet the woman might leave her alone, and that would give her time to think of ways to escape. But all she could think of was how Mum had knitted the cardigan for Great-gran's last birthday, and how she'd taught her to embroider lazy-daisies all over it. She remembered how she'd got a stitch wrong and Mum had unpicked it really carefully so as not to damage the knitting. Then there was the time that they'd had to hide it under a cushion because Great-gran had come in unexpectedly. She and Mum had got the giggles and Great-gran had giggled too even though she didn't know what they were giggling about. Best of all was when Great-gran tried it on and said it was glorious. She said that Emily's flowers were like a garden in summer and she'd worn it all through the winter, right up to the day she died. A sudden clatter of pans disturbed her thoughts. She opened her eyes and scowled as the woman turned to look at her.

'Don't look so cross,' said the woman. 'Just pretend I'm your great-gran and we'll get along fine.'

Emily couldn't help herself. Her resolve to be careful disappeared in a flash. She uncurled herself and stared at the woman. 'You've got to be joking,' she said. 'You're nothing like my great-gran.'

'But I must be like her. I fooled you into thinking I was her.'

It was true. For those first few minutes in the car park, she had been fooled, and the memory made her feel really stupid. 'You look like her but you don't behave like her. Great-gran was kind and gentle. You're mean and cruel. Besides she smelled of lavender and roses.' Emily wrinkled up her nose and sniffed. 'Everything here smells like... like rotten cabbage and sweaty armpits.'

'Careful,' said the woman. 'I told you to talk but I warned you to be careful what you say.'

Emily couldn't stop herself. 'I know what you are,' she said. 'You're a horrible, wicked witch.'

'It took you long enough to realise that,' said the woman with a sneer, 'and think yourself lucky that I don't silence you. I would too, if this wasn't getting interesting. Tell me, what do you know about witches?'

'Nothing much,' Emily stammered, 'only what I've read in fairy stories.'

'Fairy stories!' The end of the witch's nose twitched in disgust. 'Fairy stories! What have fairy stories to do with witches?'

'Well,' Emily whispered, 'they usually have a witch in them, that's all.'

Snatches of fairy tales filled Emily's head. She thought of the witch who lured Hansel and Gretel to her gingerbread house, and of all the wicked stepmothers who were really witches in disguise. Every single one of them had planned to eat, or murder a child. The terrifying detail of the stories made Emily catch her breath until she remembered that all the witches lost in the end. If she had anything to do with it, this witch would lose too. She sniffed and wiped away a tear.

'I hope you're not going to blub again,' said the witch. 'I can't stand a cry baby. Pull yourself together. Come and have some soup and then you can tell me about witches.'

Emily shook her head. She was afraid of eating anything that the witch had cooked. What if it was poisoned? What then?

The witch wagged her finger. 'Either you come and eat, or I'll make you come and eat. Which is it to be?'

Emily still hesitated.

The witch banged her wooden spoon on the table. 'Well?'

Emily had one last thing to try. Maybe Mum's positive thoughts would block the witch's spell. She closed her eyes tight, clenched her fists and concentrated. You can't make me do anything, she told herself. But it was no use. She went to the table, sat down and looked at the thick, dark soup. The curls of green steam made her retch. It looked like an evil potion, but the witch's spell forced her to pick up the spoon and eat. She choked on every mouthful, but she wasn't allowed to stop until every drop had gone.

Chapter 11

The witch pushed her empty bowl away. 'You have two choices,' she said. 'We keep the spell so that you do as you're told, or you do as you're told without it. Which is it to be?'

Emily's shoulders dropped. She was filled to the brim with foul-tasting soup. Her stomach was churning. She felt sick. She wanted her mum. Her willpower wasn't a match for the witch's evil ways. Being made to act like a robot was even worse than being turned into a statue.

'No spell,' she whispered.

The witch had proved she could over-ride her brain, but Emily wouldn't let her do it again. She'd try to do whatever the witch told her. Only she'd do something else as well. She'd watch everything the witch did. She'd discover her secrets. She'd learn some of her spells and she'd definitely find a way to escape.

'Cheer up,' said the witch in a gentle voice that didn't fool Emily at all. 'The truth is that I need your help, and once you get used to the idea I think we'll have fun. We might even be friends.'

'As if...' Emily bit back the words and stared at the witch. Never in a million years would they be friends. She tried to look away but the witch's eyes locked into hers and a strange feeling burned inside her head.

'Never in a million years!' exclaimed the witch. 'That's a pity! If we can't be friends, life is going to be very unpleasant.'

Emily gasped and looked away. The witch had read her mind! It must have happened when their eyes locked. If the witch knew what she was thinking she wouldn't be able to make plans to escape. She'd have to avoid looking into her eyes. And if she couldn't, she'd have to think different thoughts, and hope that the witch believed her. She'd have to act a part, just like she did at Drama Club. Only it wouldn't be acting. It would be for real and her life might depend on it.

'I'll try,' she stammered.

The witch's reply was sharp. 'You'll do more than try. When I show you the alternative you'll soon realise what's good for you.'

'Please,' Emily begged. 'Don't show me anything horrible. I'll be your friend. I promise.'

'Huh! Promises aren't worth a dead mouse. Look into my eyes and tell me you'll be my friend.'

Emily crossed her fingers and took a deep breath. Over and over inside her head she repeated the words. I'll be your friend. And she stared into the witch's eyes without so much as a blink. As the witch stared back, Emily could feel her poking around inside her head, as if she was seeking the truth. It made her want to bury her face in a cushion but she didn't give in. She kept her eyes wide open, and she went on thinking, I'll be your friend.

The witch narrowed her eyes. She turned her head this way and that as if she was trying to catch Emily out. 'All right,' she said at last. 'I'll give you the benefit of the doubt. Work hard, be good company, prove you really mean it and we'll see how it goes. But any more misbehaving and you won't know what's hit you. Understood?'

Emily choked and couldn't speak. All she could do was nod her head.

The witch seemed satisfied. She sat down in an armchair and closed her eyes. Emily gave a long sigh of relief. Thank goodness for Drama Club. All those practice exercises had taught her how to take on the role of different moods and different people. And now, she'd shown she could do it for real. She'd try her best to act like a really brave person. She'd fight the terror that was turning her insides to jelly. She'd bite her tongue every time she felt like answering back. She'd do as she was told, and she'd make a really good effort at being friends with the witch. But it would all be an act.

She took another deep breath and when she spoke there wasn't the slightest wobble in her voice. 'I want us to be friends,' she said. 'Really I do.'

'Good,' said the witch. 'Now you can tell me what your fairy stories say about witches.'

Emily daren't say that fairies win and witches always end up dead. She'd have to make up new stories where witches win. But the witch was waiting and she was too flustered to think of a new story. She'd just have to describe the witches and hope that this witch would be satisfied.

'Well,' she said. 'They're usually old women who wear black clothes and tall, black hats and they have…' She paused because the witch probably had an incredibly long nose under her disguise and Emily was scared of making her angry again.

'Go on,' the witch insisted. 'Tell me more.'

Emily hesitated. 'They have really long…'

'Noses.' The witch shouted the word as if she was proud of the fact. 'So they've got something right. Go on.' She leaned forward just like Emily did when Great-gran's stories got to the exciting part.

Emily's voice dropped to a whisper. 'They...also have...warts.'

'I knew it,' the witch slapped her thigh and laughed uproariously. 'But do they say why we have them?'

'No. They don't mention them. They're just there in the pictures.'

'These books have pictures,' the witch exclaimed. 'So tell me, do the witches look like me?'

Emily frowned. 'Of course they don't. You look like Great-gran, and I wish you didn't.'

The witch stared at Emily in surprise. 'I thought you'd feel more at home if I looked like her.'

'Well I don't. I want to remember Great-gran as she was, not as a horr...' She stopped herself just in time. 'Besides, I know what witches look like, and I know you're a witch, so you might as well look like one. I won't be scared. Honestly I won't.'

'You will,' said the witch.

'I won't,' said Emily.

'You will. You'll be like all the others. The sight of me makes them nervous. They make mistakes and break things. They work better if I'm in disguise. It's a darned nuisance, but I have to get the work done somehow. So I'm going to stay like this.'

Emily glanced round the room. Others! If there were others they could plan their escape together, but there was no sign of anyone else. Where could they be? She avoided the witch's eyes and pushed the thought away for later. Getting the witch to change back into herself was the first part of her plan. She had to see how magic worked. If she watched every spell

64

carefully, she might learn how to escape. She had to change the witch's mind. She thought hard for a couple of minutes and then she came up with a plan.

'Turning yourself into my great-gran was amazing,' she said. 'You must be very clever to do such powerful magic.'

The witch seemed to grow taller. She nodded her head in agreement and her face split into a most enormous grin. The sudden change made Emily hide a hint of a smile behind her hand. She'd tried flattery and the witch had responded. Well, if flattery worked once, it might work again.

'I bet no-one else in the whole world knows that spell,' she said. 'It was truly amazing. I can't imagine how you did it.'

The witch chuckled delightedly. She leaned closer and whispered. 'It was the cardigan. As soon as I touched it I knew all about your great-gran, your mum and you.'

Emily stared. 'How could a cardigan tell you that?'

'Easy,' the witch boasted. 'At least it's easy when you've spent a hundred years perfecting MRGI.'

'Whatever's that?'

'Memory Recovery from Garment Investigation,' she said. 'It's an invention of my very own. When I pick up an item of clothing I see the person who wore it, and I magic myself into their skin. I also see the people who made the garment. Your mum couldn't have imagined all the thoughts she knitted into it, and when you embroidered the flowers you stitched your secrets in it too. Luck was with me when I found it in your wardrobe. But luck isn't enough on its own, you have to be clever, and you have to be ruthless too.'

Chapter 12

The witch was undoubtedly ruthless, and Emily knew that she was clever too. Anyone who could make a car fly, anyone who could make people act like robots, anyone who could make themselves look exactly like someone else had to be very clever indeed. But the witch had made a mistake and once again Emily forgot to be careful.

'You look like my great-gran,' she said, 'but you don't act like her. Great-gran was never angry. So you got some things wrong. It's not as clever as...'

Emily's words tailed away as the witch's eyes flashed a warning. She winced and mumbled a quick apology.   But she knew she was right because the witch frowned and started to unbutton the cardigan.

'Stupid, scratchy old thing,' she said as she pulled it off. 'It told me enough to get you here, and that's all that matters. I don't need it now so I might as well burn it.'

'Please don't,' Emily begged. 'Let me have it. It was Great-gran's and it's all I have left of her.' She struggled to hold back the tears but her voice wobbled with emotion. 'If you burn it I'll be even more upset.'

The witch tossed the cardigan onto Emily's lap. 'All right. You seem to be making an effort to behave yourself. But be careful or onto the fire it will go.' She stood up and stretched. 'I feel better already and I'll feel even better when I get rid of this dumpy, little body. It squashes me up something dreadful and it slows down my spells. I think I'll change back after all. The sooner I'm in my own skin the happier I'll be.'

She began to wriggle and squirm. There was a sound like pieces of Velcro being ripped apart, and Great-gran's body began to split in two. It was the worst thing Emily had ever seen – a body tearing itself open. It was impossible to watch. She gasped and closed her eyes.

'Watch!' shouted the witch. 'You wanted me to change. Now you must watch.'

Emily pressed herself back in the chair and watched through half-closed eyes. Great-gran's body hung in loose folds, her neck drooped and her face fell in on itself. A sob caught in Emily's throat as the witch wriggled free and Great-gran's skin dropped to the floor. The witch's body grew taller and thinner, her grey hair loosened and lengthened. Her chin grew pointed. Her nose grew longer. A wart erupted on the end of it and some stiff, black hairs sprouted out. But what scared Emily most of all was the long, black fingernail that grew on the first finger of her left hand. It grew and grew until it looked like the talon of some terrifying, prehistoric monster.

The witch waved it so close to Emily that it caught her cheek. 'Take a good look at this,' she said. 'Mind your manners and do as you're told or you'll find out what it can do.'

The sudden scratch made Emily gasp. Her hand flew up to soothe the stinging, and when she saw that her fingers were red with blood, her tears flowed again.

'I warned you,' said the witch. 'I will not tolerate tears. Dry them up or I'll give you something to cry about.'

It took the most enormous effort for Emily to stop crying. The scratch from the hideous fingernail was stinging so much that her cheek began to throb. What if it was poisoned and the poison was seeping into her bloodstream?

'Please can I clean it?' she begged.

'Clean it! Why on earth would you want to clean it? It'll heal soon enough,' snapped the witch. 'I haven't poisoned you if that's what you think. So pull yourself together and tell me what I look like now.'

Emily swallowed hard and struggled to find her voice. 'You look like a witch in a story book.'

'That's impossible,' screeched the witch. 'I'm not like any other witch, and I'm definitely not a witch in a story book. I'm a real witch. I'm one of the most powerful witches in the world, and don't you forget it.' She turned her profile towards Emily. 'Take a good look and tell me, are the witches in your story books as handsome as me?'

Emily shook her head, and although she stared, she managed to avoid looking into the witch's eyes. How could she possibly be called handsome? None of the witches she'd seen in pictures were as ugly as this witch. Her wrinkled face had a greenish tinge, her eyes were bloodshot and her nose stuck out like a pan-handle. Her scraggy hair looked like greasy string and her long, bony fingers had unbelievably filthy nails.

'No,' she said at last. 'They don't look as ba... I mean they don't look as handsome as you and their warts are never as big as yours.'

The witch laughed. 'Well they wouldn't be, would they? Only members of The Grand High Council have warts bigger than mine.'

It was hard to imagine a wart bigger than the one on the end of this witch's nose, and Emily couldn't imagine why anyone would want one. 'What's special about warts?' she asked. 'I mean they're not exactly pretty.'

'Pretty,' snorted the witch. 'Why would I want to be pretty? Pretty things are for fairies. No. Warts are marks of distinction. Warts are Badges of Honour. You have to be a witch for a hundred years before you get even a tiny one.'

Her long fingers pushed back a strand of hair from her cheek and she pointed to a small, brown wart next to her ear. 'See this, it's not much to look at but I had to earn it. It was my reward for studying hard and passing CMW Exam 100.'

'CMW?' asked Emily. 'What's that??'

'Council of Malevolent Witches,' explained the witch. 'Witches aren't just born, you know. You have to prove yourself worthy of the name. It helps if your father's a malevolent wizard, like mine. It's even better if your mother's a malevolent witch as well. Unfortunately my mother was just ordinary.'

Her nose quivered with disgust as she added, 'Very ordinary. She tried to stop me from being a witch but my father soon...' She paused. 'No need to go into that. I wanted to be a witch so nothing she said could stop me. Watch this. It was the first magic I ever performed. I was just a tiny tot in a high chair at the time.'

She pointed at the fireplace and clicked her long black fingernail against her thumb. The fire died immediately. When she clicked again, the logs leapt back into life, yellow, orange and red flames curling up the chimney. A slow smile spread across her face.

'That's when I knew I was destined to be a witch. It's the power you see. It takes over your life and nothing else matters. You have to keep inventing new spells. Then, if you pass your exams they give you a wart and another hundred years.'

'But what happens if your spells don't work and you fail your exams?'

The witch chortled. 'You die. The end. It's hilarious when it happens to someone else.' Her laughter faded as if she'd suddenly realised that it wouldn't be funny if it happened to her.

'I have to perfect my latest spell, but I'm running out of time. That's why I need you to cook and clean. You have to do some sewing too, but more of that later. I was telling you about my warts.'

Emily looked round at the chaotic mess. The thought of putting her hands into the filthy sink made her feel queasy. And why should she do it anyway?

'Why can't you clean up by clicking your finger?' she asked.

'Because I need to save all my magic power for the new spell. And that's why I don't want to waste it on you. Now you know why I need you to behave.'

Emily stored that little snippet of information away in her brain. One of these days it might come in useful.

Chapter 13

The witch went on bragging about her Badges of Honour. She lifted up her chin and pointed to another wart. 'I got this for passing Exam 200, and this one,' she touched a large pink wart just above her grey hairy eyebrow, 'was for Exam 300.' She leaned towards Emily so that the enormous, red wart on the end of her nose was right in front of Emily's eyes.

'This was for Exam 400. Four hundred years in the service of Malevolent Witchery, for contributing to the downfall of Benevolent Wizards, Benevolent Witches, Fairy Folk and all those goody-goodies who strive to make the world a happy place. Happy,' she snorted. 'What's the point in being happy? I never heard anything so boring in my life.'

She twiddled the bristles that sprouted from the biggest wart. 'And there's one of these for every decade beyond four hundred.'

Emily tried to count them, but they were packed so close that she couldn't tell if there were eight or nine. 'Wow!' She forced herself to sound impressed. 'Does that mean you're nearly five hundred? I didn't know anyone could live that long, not even a witch.'

'I'm four hundred and ninety-nine.' For a moment the witch looked proud, then her face crumpled and she sat down heavily. 'Soon it will be time for Exam 500, the most important exam of all. Every answer has to be correct and it's so diabolically difficult that practically every witch fails. That's why there aren't many really old witches left. But I'll show them. I worked out a way of passing when I sat Exam 100 and I'll pass this one too, no doubt about it.'

She heaved a great sigh. 'But I have to perform a spectacular new spell at The Festival of Malevolent Witchery. If I manage that I'll become the thirteenth and last witch on The Grand High Council of Malevolent Witches.'

'What does that mean?' asked Emily.

'It means I won't ever have to take exams again. It means I'll be able to concentrate on the most important spell of all.'

'What's that?' Emily asked.

'That's for me to know and you to wonder,' snapped the witch. 'You're getting too inquisitive by half.'

'Sorry,' said Emily, 'but can you tell me what happens if you fail?'

The witch's green-tinged face turned pale. 'I told you, it's the end. But I can't let that happen. There's a spell to perfect. I must concentrate and you must help me.'

'But I can't do spells.' Emily glanced round the room. Her heart sank at the terrible mess. If she had to clean up she wouldn't know where to start, besides, the witch had mentioned sewing, and that was far more appealing.

'I thought you wanted me to sew,' she said. 'Will I have time to sew as well as cook and clean?'

The witch looked doubtful. 'Probably not. Doing housework would waste your time. You can sew and I'll get someone else to clean and cook. Then, if you behave yourself you can help with the spells. I saw you cooking with your mum so you should be able to mix ingredients, stir potions and stop the cauldron from boiling over.'

She got up and twiddled a knob on a television screen above the fireplace. 'Watch this. It's the last Festival and these are the finalists. They all failed. That's why the thirteenth chair still needs filling. Take a good look at the costumes. That's where you come in.'

'I don't understand.'

The witch gave an exasperated sigh. 'The costume,' she repeated. 'I have to have a costume. When I perform my spell at the Festival, I have to make a grand entrance. Twenty per cent of the marks are for stage presence and presentation. So I need an amazing costume. It has to be more original than anything any other witch has ever worn. From the moment I saw your embroidery I knew that you could do it. Tomorrow you must start to sew.'

'You mean you want me to embroider flowers on your costume?'

The witch turned and towered over Emily. 'Flowers!' she screeched. 'Of course I don't want flowers. Flowers are for fairies. Flowers would turn me into a laughing stock. Think, girl, think!'

Emily couldn't think. Fear drove every thought out of her head. She covered her eyes to block out the witch's angry face.

The witch sank back into her chair. She was no longer screeching, but her voice was harsh and impatient. 'I mean magic symbols, swords and pentacles, and witchy things like spider webs, witches on broomsticks and bats. Flowers indeed!'

Terrified of forgetting the list, Emily went over it in her head. She didn't even know what a pentacle was, and in any case, she only knew how to sew flowers.

Lazy-daisy, stem stitch and French knots were easy, but she hadn't a clue how to embroider a witch on a broomstick.

'I might manage the embroidery,' she said, 'but someone else will have to make the costume.'

The witch frowned. 'What do you mean?'

'I mean I don't know how to sew a costume.'

The witch's eyes flashed. Emily could see her finger twitching. She had to think of something to calm her down. 'We could always design it together and you could get one of the Fancy Dress shops to make it for you.'

'No way.' The witch thumped her fist on the chair arm. 'No-one outside these walls must know anything about it. You'll have to manage. It's a good job I never throw anything away. I have a trunk full of my mother's clothes.' She gave a little chuckle. 'For the first time in my life I'm glad she wasn't a witch. There's no magic attached to any of her things so you can do what you want with them.'

Emily shrugged. She'd watched Great-gran making dresses and it had looked really difficult. She'd helped Mum to make costumes for school plays, but they hadn't done much sewing. Mostly they'd fastened things together with safety pins and sticky tape. If anyone looked closely they could see they weren't well made. But when they were up on the stage no one could tell. Maybe she could manage after all.

'I'll try,' she said, 'but I'll have to make a list of all the things I need.'

The witch sighed. 'That means a shopping trip and I don't have time.'

'Well,' said Emily. 'You won't have to bother if you make your costume by magic. Why don't you do that?'

'Because,' said the witch, 'I'm competing against other witches. They'll try to sabotage my chances. If an innocent little girl makes my costume they won't be able to destroy it. That's why you've got to do it for me. Let's make a bargain. Do your best work. Make it absolutely amazing, and on the day I win, I'll send you home.'

The thought of going home made Emily's heart leap, but could she trust the witch to keep her word? She looked up and the witch's eyes locked into hers. There it was again, that horrible poking sensation deep inside her head. She tried to change her thoughts but it was too late. She simply couldn't lower her eyes.

'I know what you're thinking,' said the witch, 'you think you can't trust me, but when I join The Grand High Council I won't need you. I'll have servants to do my bidding and I'll send you home.' She grabbed Emily by the hand, and peered into her eyes. 'Well, is it a deal?'

Emily told the truth. 'I want to go home, but you won't let me, so I'll have to do what you ask. Only what happens when they start looking for me? You're going to be in awful trouble when they find us.'

The witch let go of Emily's hand and doubled over with laughter. 'Find us! Find you! Find me! Who do you think is going to find me? My hiding place is the strongest, safest spell of all. If it weren't, the other witches would find me and steal my spells. No, not even The Grand High Witch herself can find me.'

Chapter 14

A frown creased the witch's forehead. 'The other witches want to find me because they know my spells are the best. But they're no match for me. The only danger is from Benevolent Wizards. They're always poking their pathetic, little noses into witchy business. They want to rid the world of Malevolent Witchery. But no,' she shook her head and grinned. 'They can't get the better of Ammonia B Clickfinger.'

So that was her name. Emily had heard of ammonia, she thought it was a poisonous sort of gas, and after the trick with the fire it was obvious why she was called Clickfinger.

'What's the B for?' she asked.

'None of your business,' Ammonia snapped. 'Don't you know that your full name can be used to cast spells against you. You should never tell it to anyone. That, Miss Emily Elizabeth Carmichael, is why I have power over you.'

Emily's mouth fell open. 'But...but I didn't tell you my name.'

'You didn't need to,' said Ammonia. 'You embroidered it into the cardigan along with the flowers.'

Emily looked up in surprise. She tried to put the B out of her mind, but it wouldn't go away.

'Don't you dare try to find my middle name,' Ammonia yelled. 'They're still looking for the last girl who tried.' She laughed hysterically. 'But guess what? They'll never find her.'

The clock struck two and Ammonia's laughter stopped abruptly.

'No more interruptions,' she snapped. 'The day's half gone and apart from finding you I've nothing to show for it.' She threw a bag of peas at Emily. 'Make yourself useful, pod those while I work on my spell.'

Emily caught the bag. 'What shall I put them in?' she asked.

Ammonia wasn't listening. She was stirring a pot on the stove, adding drops of purple liquid from a bottle and muttering to herself. She seemed to have forgotten that Emily existed.

Cautiously Emily tiptoed to the kitchen, found an empty pan, returned to her chair and tipped the peapods onto her knee. She split the first pod with her thumbnail and dropped the peas into the tin. They landed with a tinkling sound, bouncing and rolling until they nestled together. Last time I podded peas, she thought, Great-gran was peeling potatoes and Mum was roasting chicken.

Back home Mum would be baking. They always baked on Saturday afternoons, trying out new recipes, or making her favourite chocolate brownies. She imagined Mum tying on her apron, and lifting down the flour bin that only she could reach. Only she wouldn't be doing that. She'd be frantic with worry, the way she'd been when Dad hadn't come home at the usual time. Emily still had nightmares about that, about Mum pacing up and down, looking at her watch, ringing his mobile over and over and getting no answer. About phoning the police and the hours they'd waited with Mum getting more and more anxious. And worst of all, the police coming to tell them there'd been an accident.

Mum had been hysterical. She'd flung herself on the bed and wailed like a wounded animal. It was the only time Emily had seen her like that and she didn't want to see her like that again. But that's how she'd be now, and she'd be alone because there was no Great-gran to comfort her.

She could remember her, white-faced, sobbing and breaking her heart. Now her own heart was breaking. It felt as if a giant fist was crushing it into a million pieces. For her mum's sake she had to get home and she mustn't make things worse by annoying the witch. She kept wiping her tears, but she couldn't stop them falling. She went on shelling peas, peering through misty eyes, trying to think of ways to escape, trying not to think about the girl who would never be found.

Above the ticking of the clock and Ammonia's muttering she heard a sound. It was faint at first, like children calling to one another across a playground. They sounded excited, not at all scared or unhappy. Perhaps Ammonia hadn't treated them badly after all. She glanced at Ammonia.

The witch didn't seem to notice the noise, but as the sound grew louder she began to curse. 'Dratted tourists. How am I supposed to concentrate?'

There was a clatter of feet and a group of children burst into the room. They came as if from nowhere, like shadows ·stealing through walls, jostling and passing through the furniture as if it simply didn't exist. Emily gasped as a girl walked right through her. She reached out to grab a hand but her fingers closed on nothing but air. A teacher followed, urging them to slow down, telling them to stand still and listen. Emily

78

listened too, hoping to hear something that would help her to escape.

'Gylen Castle,' began the teacher, 'was a stronghold of the MacDougall clan. It was built in 1587, but in 1647 it was besieged by General Leslie and his Covenanter Army. They burned the castle and killed everyone who was sheltering in it.'

Emily listened as the teacher went on and on. Ammonia covered her ears. The children began to get restless. A boy with very fair hair came towards Emily. He reached out as if to touch her cheek.

'I know you're there,' he whispered.

Emily's heart leapt. She whispered her name. She tried to tell the boy what had happened, but he didn't seem to hear. 'Please,' she said, 'please don't go.'

He screwed up his eyes as if he was peering into mist. He waved his hand, cutting through her face again and again. Then he gave a puzzled frown and shrugged.

'Don't go,' she said again.

But the teacher was calling the children to order. The boy turned away and there was nothing she could do to stop him.

'Be careful on the stairs,' said the teacher. 'Keep in single file and no pushing. Once we're outside we'll have to hurry. We mustn't miss the ferry.'

Emily jumped to her feet and tried to follow but the bookshelves blocked her way. She called after them, desperate to be noticed. 'Wait for me. Let me come too.' But although she shouted at the top of her voice there was no response.

Ammonia laughed. 'Stupid girl,' she said. 'They can't hear you. They're in another dimension, back in that boring world of yours.'

Emily clung to the bookshelf, listening intently, dreading the moment when the cheerful chatter faded away. If only she could pass through the wall she was sure the teacher would help her. She gritted her teeth, set her shoulder against the shelf and pushed.

'Forget it,' said Ammonia. 'They're visiting the ruined castle and that's all they can see. They can't see either of us.'

'But that boy, the one with the fair hair, he knew I was here.'

Ammonia looked startled. 'Then the sooner he's away from here the better. I don't want his sort sniffing out my secrets. But I don't think I need to worry. He'll just think he saw a ghost. He won't have a clue who you really are.'

Well, thought Emily. He may not have a clue but I have two. I'm in Gylen Castle. I don't know where it is, but if they have to catch a ferry it must be on an island. She stored that information away inside her head, and when the time came she would use it.

Chapter 15

The shouts and laughter died away. Emily snuggled into Great-gran's cardigan. Ammonia had called it horrible and scratchy. But it wasn't. It was soft and warm and it still smelled of lavender. She watched the fire making patterns as the logs burned and crumbled, but all the time, her mind was racing. Tomorrow she would have to start making Ammonia's costume, and she was scared that she wouldn't be able to do it.

'Please,' she began.

Ammonia slammed her spoon down. 'What?' she demanded. 'What's the problem now?'

'Please let me go home,' said Emily. 'There must be someone else who can sew. I'm worried about my mum. She'll be looking for me. So will the police. They'll put a picture of me on television. I'll be in the newspapers in the morning. You think they'll never find me but...'

Ammonia cut her off with an impatient wave of her hand. 'I know they won't find you because they won't be looking. Back in your world you're still in the car park so there's no point in worrying about your mum.'

Emily looked at the clock on the wall. 'I don't understand. I can't be in two places at once. It's half past three. I've been here for four hours. Time hasn't stopped.'

'Ah! But that's my clock and my time,' said the witch. 'Your time is on your watch.'

Emily pushed back her sleeve and stared at the digital numbers. She blinked and stared again. Her watch showed 11.27. But what did it mean? How could there be different times for different people?

'So are you saying that my mum doesn't even know I've disappeared?'

'Hasn't a clue!' Ammonia laughed and clutched her sides as if it was the biggest joke in the whole world. 'You could be here forever and she wouldn't even miss you.'

A horrible empty feeling filled Emily's chest. She struggled to understand. If her time had stopped, and Mum's time had stopped too, when would it start again? Would it ever start again? And if it didn't, would she stay here forever? Would she stay the same age and never get any older? If only she was at home with Mum. But if Ammonia was right, Mum wouldn't be at home. She'd still be in the supermarket. She'd be there forever. It didn't make sense. She looked at her watch again. She tapped it and wiggled it about on her wrist. She even tried clicking her fingers at it, but the numbers didn't change. No matter what she tried, they showed 11.27. And how could Mum fail to miss her? The empty feeling rose up in her throat and threatened to choke her.

'I want my mum,' she wailed.

Ammonia jumped to her feet and spoke through clenched teeth. 'For the last time, forget your mother. Mention her again and I'll...'

'Don't.' Emily cowered away from the witch. 'Don't do anything. Please. I'm trying. I really am. But I'm confused and you keep scaring me. I never know what you're going to do next. Sometimes you're friendly, but then you get all angry and...and witchified.'

'You're a fine one to talk,' said Ammonia. 'Proper feisty little madam you are. But I'm in charge so you'll have to get used to my moods. I'm certainly not going to get used to yours. As for the time thing, all you need to know is that your mum won't miss you. That's a vital part of the magic. If every parent missed the children I've captured the country would be in uproar. The fuss they make when one child goes missing is ridiculous. Imagine the hullaballoo if they knew I had dozens of them.'

Emily gulped. She glanced round the room for signs of other children but there were none. If Ammonia was speaking the truth they must be somewhere. Sooner or later she would meet them, and when she did, they could plan their escape together. Only they'd have to be careful not to make Ammonia suspicious – and they'd have to learn some magic.

'When I go back,' Emily asked, 'will it still be 11.27? And will my time start up again?'

'Yes, if I send you back. But why are you asking?'

'I'm trying to get it straight in my head, that's all,' said Emily. 'So, my being here is like having another life. It's time that I wouldn't normally have.'

Ammonia nodded. 'I guess that's right. I hadn't really thought about it.'

A plan was forming in Emily's mind. She sat up straight and smiled. 'Then I want to make the most of it. Great-gran told me to learn from every opportunity. So that's what I'm going to do. It's not every girl who gets to help a witch. I'll make the costume, but I want to help with your spells as well.' She forced another smile. 'I want to learn magic. I can't think of anything I'd rather do.'

Ammonia crouched down and stared into Emily's eyes, but Emily was ready. Now that she had a plan it was easy to put on an excited act. She made her eyes sparkle and she thought what fun it would be to learn real magic.

'Well. This is a turn up for the spell books,' said Ammonia. 'Does that mean there'll be no more whining?'

'I'm not a whiner.' Emily crossed her fingers because she knew that when she was in a bad mood she could whine like anything. She paused and thought for a moment. 'At least I'll try my best. But I'm like you. Sometimes my temper gets the better of me.'

The witch threw back her head and hooted with laughter. 'If you weren't so blooming awkward I might start to like you,' she said. 'You've got the guts to stand up for yourself and you're honest. I must say it's a relief to know you're serious about co-operating. From the way you've been behaving I could have sworn you were going to be nothing but trouble.'

Emily shrugged. 'That's because I was worried about my mum, but if she isn't going to miss me, she'll be fine. Now I understand about the extra time I won't miss school or anything.'

'It seems I made a good choice after all,' said Ammonia. 'You can embroider and you're a careful worker. I could tell that by the way you sewed the buttons on the cardigan. They're really neat with no dangly ends and the colour of the thread is a perfect match. Besides, the fact that you're so small is a real bonus. You'll be able to creep into spaces that are too small for me.'

Emily gasped. She was brave about most things, but ever since she'd spent three hours trapped in a lift in the dark, she'd suffered from claustrophobia. Small spaces totally freaked her out. She was so horrified that she couldn't speak for a whole minute.

'But if you're so clever,' she blurted out, 'why can't you make yourself little then you can go into small spaces?'

Ammonia scowled and raised her finger. 'Because I need my energy for more important things,' she snapped. 'And there you go again. Just when I thought we'd come to an understanding you go and spoil it. It's not your place to question me. You'll do whatever I tell you to do. And you'll go wherever I want you to go.'

Emily's voice began to shake. 'But not small spaces, anywhere except small spaces.' Her voice rose to a scream and she started to sob hysterically.

Ammonia's eyes narrowed. She shouted above the sound of Emily's weeping. 'Stop it, or I'll stop you for good.'

Emily buried her face in her hands. She struggled to control her sobs, but her chest heaved and her whole body shook.

The witch drummed her fingers on the table. She crossed the room and grabbed Emily by the chin. 'Look at me,' she ordered, 'and look at this.' She waved her long black fingernail under Emily's nose. 'I think it's time to show you what it can do.'

Chapter 16

Emily, with her chin held in a vice-like grip, closed her eyes so that she couldn't see Ammonia's hideous fingernail.

'Open your eyes,' the witch commanded. 'When you see what my clickfinger can do you'll be too scared to disobey.'

Quick as a blink she swung round and clicked at a spider that was resting in a web above the mantelpiece. Instantly it turned into a bluebottle. Its wings caught in the web and it buzzed frantically as it struggled to free itself.

Ammonia grinned triumphantly. 'That's my very own Transformation Spell. That pesky spider has been capturing flies for years. Now it knows what it feels like.

She came close to Emily and whispered, 'I do it to children too. If they annoy me I turn them into something else. Watching them change is hilarious. Seeing them sprout feathers or extra legs has me in stitches.'

Emily's hands flew to her mouth. She gulped and tried to swallow the nauseous feeling. It was worse than she'd imagined. The children she'd hoped to find weren't children at all.

'It's too horrible,' she gasped. 'Tell me it isn't true. Or at least tell me that you change them back.'

'I can't tell you that because it is true. It's possible to change them back, but I don't usually bother. It's a tricky business called Reverse Transformation, but it's a two-part spell and if I miss the second bit they go home. That's fine for them but it's no fun for me. I'd rather keep them here so I can gloat over them when I'm feeling miserable. No, if I want another helper it's quicker to go out and find one.'

'You mean they stay here?'

'Mostly,' said the witch, 'but if they're troublesome I use the Elimination Spell.' She clicked at the bluebottle. The buzzing stopped. The bluebottle dropped like a stone. It landed on Emily's lap and disappeared in a tiny swirl of dust. 'Then they're dead. Their time starts again and their parents report them missing.' She rubbed her hands together and grinned. 'Of course, they never find them because there's nothing left to find. A puff of dust and they're gone.'

'But that's horrible,' Emily shouted. 'That's the worst thing I've heard in my life. It's monstrous. It's murder.'

The witch came closer. Her face turned purple, her eyes flashed and her long black fingernail twitched.

Something huge and heavy seemed to drop into Emily's tummy. 'But...' she gulped, 'you wouldn't do that to me. You need me to make your costume and you said we could be friends.'

'Friends!' Ammonia screeched. 'Forget it. How can we be friends? You question everything. You answer back. You're more trouble than you're worth.' She turned away and scratched her head as if she was at her wit's end.

Emily wanted to beg and plead, but she daren't open her mouth. She held her breath, dreading what the witch would do next.

When Ammonia eventually spoke she was calmer, but her voice was cold and hard. 'You're right. I do need you. Only understand this. If you want me to keep my side of the bargain you'll have to stop losing your temper, and you'd better remember what happened to the spider.'

Emily knew she could never forget the spider. She huddled in the chair and shivered. She thought about time standing still, and whatever Ammonia said, she was sure that her mum was missing her.

'Stop brooding and make yourself useful.' Ammonia threw a drawing pad and a pack of felt pens onto Emily's lap. 'Draw some ideas for my costume, and make sure they're spectacular.'

Emily's mind was as blank as the sheet of paper. She hadn't a clue where to start. All she knew was that the embroidery had to be big and bold. If Ammonia was going to stand on a stage there would be an audience, and if the audience couldn't see the embroidery there was no point in doing it. She looked up and tried to imagine something different from the dull black clothes that the witch was wearing.

Ammonia was muttering as she sorted through a jumble of papers. Emily could tell she was still angry. It showed in the way she screwed up papers and aimed them at the fire. Emily strained to hear what she was saying. She could pick out odd words, words that Ammonia spat out angrily, words like vengeance, punish, and one that she didn't understand – retribution. But without the words that came between, they didn't make sense at all.

She drew the things that Ammonia had mentioned, but she struggled with witches on broomsticks, and she still didn't know what a pentacle was. She was about to ask when something made her stop. Ammonia had slipped her hand inside the neck of her dress and was pulling out a locket on a chain. She opened it and stretched out her arms as if she was pulling a thread between her hands, a thread so slender that it seemed to be invisible. Then she wound it round her finger, returned it to the locket, and popped it back inside her dress.

'Time,' Ammonia groaned. 'I'm running out of time.'

Emily looked at her watch. It was still showing 11.27. Running out of time didn't make sense. If Ammonia could manage time she had all the time in the world. She glanced up at the clock on the wall, and before she could look away, Ammonia's eyes locked into hers.

Immediately the witch answered the question that was on her mind. 'I'm locked into dratted CMW time,' she fumed, 'and there isn't enough of it. On top of that I've lost something important.'

She shuffled through the piles of papers so hurriedly that one sheet fell off the table, drifted across the room and into the fire. She screeched, rushed to pull it out and tried to stamp out the flames. Too late! Most of the paper had turned to ash. She fell on her knees and stared at the one remaining fragment.

'Pond slime and pig poo,' she cursed. 'That's a week's work wasted. I've too much to do and not enough time to do it. Come with me and we'll find someone to keep the place tidy. It's time to try Reverse Transformation.'

Ammonia banged her stick on the floor in the corner of the room. There was a rumbling sound as a section of shelves slid away to reveal a door. She fumbled in her pocket and brought out an enormous bunch of keys.

Emily edged closer to see which key the witch would choose, but all she saw was a flash of silver. As the door swung open, a stench of animal poo and rotting vegetables hit her like a slap in the face. Horrified, she took a step backwards.

'No you don't,' said Ammonia with an evil grin. 'You've got to see this. Welcome to my zoo.'

Emily hesitated, but a hefty push sent her stumbling into a wire cage. A startled squeak came from inside, and all around were sounds of scurrying feet and rustling hay. It was as if hundreds of small creatures were dashing for cover. The silence that followed was deep and the very air was heavy with feelings of pain and anguish. Emily almost fainted from the weight of it. She closed her smarting eyes against the acrid air. She coughed and retched, certain that at any moment she'd be sick.

'Pull yourself together, ' Ammonia shouted. 'Come and help.'

The smell was so foul that Emily could taste it. She closed her lips and took the smallest breaths through her nose. Somehow she had to overcome the feeling of nausea. If she didn't, there was no telling what the witch would do. She forced her eyes open and peered into the dimly lit room. All she could see were cages – cages hanging from rafters, cages piled on benches, cages stacked on the straw-littered floor. Nothing moved. Whatever lived in the cages was either dead, or hiding.

Chapter 17

Ammonia stomped round the room, looking into the cages and angrily dismissing each one with a comment. 'He's too slow. She never stops crying. I can't bear the sight of him. Definitely not her.'

Eventually she stopped by a large pen. 'Joanna Blackstock might do,' she said. 'She was a good worker, but the greedy brat ate the chocolate off the top of a cake, left her teeth marks in it too. Still, if I can stop her from eating too much, she should do nicely.'

Lifting up her skirt she climbed into the pen, kicked at a mound of hay, grabbed a fat pink leg and pulled. There was an angry squeal, but the pig didn't budge. Ammonia prodded through the straw with her stick. With every prod the squeals grew more and more indignant.

Emily winced each time the pig squealed. She willed it to move before Ammonia decided it would be easier to eliminate it. Prod, prod, prod. Squeal, squeal, squeal. Still the pig didn't move.

'Greedy beast,' Ammonia yelled. 'You've eaten so much you can't get up, and bother, I've forgotten the Reverse Transformation spray. Emily, go and get it. It's in the green bottles on the bottom shelf to the left of the fireplace.'

Emily ran back and searched through dozens of containers. It took ages to find a green one. She rushed back to Ammonia, dreading a reprimand for being slow. To her relief, the witch grabbed the spray without complaining.

'Get in here,' she said to Emily. 'Move the straw. I need to see more skin.'

Emily climbed into the pen and shuddered as a lump of pig poo squashed under her feet. All she could see of the pig was a huge pink bottom at one end and a grubby snout at the other. Quickly she moved the filthy straw aside and when more of the pig was exposed Ammonia sprayed it.

Emily scrambled out of the pen as the pig disappeared under a heap of green foam. Her eyes widened as bubbles began to fill the pen. Ammonia backed away and tried to climb out, but she caught her foot on the rail and at that moment there was an explosion. Green foam flew in every direction. It landed on Ammonia, on Emily, and on all the nearby cages. It covered the floor. It splattered the ceiling. It rose into the air and fell down like hideous green snow. It stank like pig poo, and when the last speck settled, an evil-smelling mist rose into the air. Through the last skeins of it, Emily caught the briefest glimpse of a very large girl. The startled eyes registered shock as they connected with Emily's. Then the girl was gone.

Ammonia had landed on her back with her legs in the air. She shrieked and thrashed about like a toddler in a tantrum. When she finally struggled to her feet she whacked the pen with her stick. 'That's torn it,' she fumed. 'Now I'll have to find someone else.'

She pushed Emily out of her way. 'Check the labels. Find James Henry Watson. He might do.'

Although Emily pinched her nose it didn't block out the stink. She walked along the row of cages, gasping as she read the names on the labels. Her eyes blurred with tears. She couldn't read any more. Could it be true? Could every one of these cages hold something that had once been a child? Could all these children have been transformed into creatures simply because they'd annoyed Ammonia?

'Found him,' Ammonia shouted. 'Come and meet James Henry Watson.' She opened a cage and stuck her long nose inside. 'Come on out,' she wheedled. 'I know you're there.'

There was a slight movement among the cabbage leaves in the corner of the cage, but James didn't come out.

'Last chance,' snapped Ammonia. 'Reverse Transformation or Elimination. Which is it to be?'

Emily held her breath, hoping that whatever James was, he'd have the sense to come out. Slowly, very slowly, two tentacles appeared and a long slimy body moved along the midrib of a well-chewed leaf.

Emily shuddered. It was an enormous black slug, and she couldn't stand slugs.

'Get him out,' ordered Ammonia, 'and put him on a tray.'

If he'd been a snail, Emily could have picked him up by the shell. If he'd been a worm she wouldn't have minded at all, but a slimy slug was another matter.

'I'll turn you into one if you don't get a move on,' said Ammonia.

So Emily put her hand in the cage and slid her fingers under the leaf that held the slug.

'Not the leaf,' Ammonia snarled. 'The slug, nothing but the slug.'

Emily braced herself. As soon as she touched the slug, it drew in its tentacles and its body hunched up into a fat, black blob. She cringed as her fingers closed on its sticky body. She had to remind herself that it wasn't a slug. It was James Henry Watson. She lifted him out of the cage and tried to put him on the tray, but he was stuck to her fingers. She pushed him off with her other hand. Then she ran to the sink to wash away the slime.

The witch scowled and her chin jutted out angrily. 'You, my girl, must learn to obey orders without being squeamish. Mark my words, there'll be worse things to do than touch a slug.'

Emily carried the tray at arm's length, keeping the black blob as far away from her face as possible. As she followed Ammonia into the other room, she looked round for clues, anything that might help when the time came to escape. She watched Ammonia select the largest key, fit it into the keyhole and turn it three times. And she noticed a shiny mark where the witch had banged the floor to slide the shelves away.

'Last chance,' said Ammonia as she took the tray and placed it on the floor. 'You know what'll happen if you mess up again. Don't you?'

The slug's tentacles poked out. Its body grew longer and thinner. The eyes on the ends of the tentacles looked up at Ammonia and the head nodded slowly. Ammonia held up the bottle and sprayed.

Emily didn't know what to expect because the spell had gone wrong when Joanna was sprayed. The girl had disappeared and Emily was afraid that she'd been eliminated. Now, her whole body tensed. She held her breath and clenched her fists as the slug began to squirm. She watched as green froth bubbled up all over it. Her eyes widened as it grew and grew until, with a flash, a bang and a billow of green smoke, it exploded.

At the very same moment, Ammonia clapped her hands and shouted, 'Cut.'

Emily squinted into the smoke. When it cleared the slug had gone and a boy was lying in its place. Although the whole procedure was enough to make anyone faint from shock, Emily couldn't help thinking that she'd seen something remarkable.

'Wow!' she exclaimed. 'That was incredible, but why did you say 'cut'?'

'Because if I hadn't, I'd have lost him.' Ammonia leant over James, laughing delightedly. 'Incredible is the perfect word. It's such fun I should do it more often. It was my project for CMW Exam 300.' She pointed to the shiny pink wart above her eyebrow. 'This was my reward.'

Emily was barely listening. She was watching James. He hadn't started to move and worry was making her tummy turn over. She couldn't even see him breathing. Had something gone wrong with the spell? Her heart raced and she clutched the chair to stop herself from falling over.

'Please,' she begged, 'tell me he isn't dead.'

Chapter 18

Ammonia prodded James with her stick. 'Of course he's not dead. He's in shock, that's all. He'll come round soon. And when he does, he'll be hungry, so light the gas under the soup.'

By the time the soup was bubbling, James was stirring. He opened his eyes and blinked. He tried to sit up, but immediately toppled over.

'Put his soup on the table,' ordered Ammonia.

Emily poured the soup into a bowl and carried it to the table. James tried to stand but he wobbled and fell to his knees. He tried to grab a chair arm but he missed and fell flat on his face. Emily rushed to help him.

'Stop!' Ammonia shouted. 'If he can't pull himself together he can go back to being a slug. He's got ten minutes to get to the table, and that's it.'

Emily nibbled her fingernails as she watched James. There was no sign of movement. Her gaze flitted from him to the clock and back again. Time ticked away. Soon there were only five minutes left. She daren't speak out loud, but inside her head she was telling him to hurry. With only two minutes to spare, he rolled onto his knees, crawled across the floor, grabbed the table leg and pulled himself onto a chair. He started to eat, slowly at first, but soon he was wolfing the soup down as if he hadn't eaten for years. When he'd used the last piece of bread to wipe his bowl clean, he lifted his head. For less than a second his eyes met Emily's, but it was long enough to tell her that he was absolutely terrified.

'Right,' said Ammonia as she sat opposite James. 'Let's get a few things straight. 'No refusals, no mistakes, no accidents. I've got a room full of potential helpers and I'm prepared to use every single one of them. Do as you're told and I won't need to, but annoy me just once and I'll replace you. One mistake and it's Elimination. Understood?'

James nodded his head, but he didn't look at Ammonia and he didn't look at Emily either.

'And it's Transformation for you.' Ammonia grinned and looked at Emily through half-closed eyes. 'I like to fit the creature to the personality so yours will be a fighter.' After a moment's thought she began to laugh. 'Devil's coach horse, that's what you'll be. I've never had one before. It'll make a nice change from slugs and worms and timid little beasties. No cabbage leaves for you my girl. Worms and woodlice, that's what you'll eat, fat juicy worms and crunchy little woodlice. That'll teach you not to be squeamish.'

Emily's tummy turned over. She retched at the thought of swallowing worms, and she covered her mouth to stop from being sick.

'Don't worry,' Ammonia laughed. 'It'll only happen if you misbehave.'

The witch picked up the mist sprayer and cursed because it was almost empty. She went to the shelf and rummaged among the bottles 'I must have used it all,' she muttered, 'and I haven't time to make any more. Still, if you two behave yourselves I won't need to bother. Now get to bed. I need you ready for work in the morning.'

Emily didn't expect to sleep. She was far too worried for that. But time away from Ammonia would allow her to think. Besides, she wouldn't have to hold her tongue and avoid Ammonia's eyes. She scanned the room, wondering where the bedrooms were. Was there another secret doorway behind one of the bookcases? It was impossible to tell. She stood up, waiting for Ammonia to point the way.

'Not so fast,' snapped the witch. 'I can't let you go without a guard.'

'I don't need a guard,' Emily exclaimed. 'I'm not going anywhere. I told you, I want to learn to be a witch. I can't wait to start learning spells. Anyway, I can't see a door or a window so I couldn't escape even if I wanted to.'

'Escape! Hah! I know you can't escape. That's not the reason for a guard. It's to stop you poking your nose into things that don't concern you. I had more than enough of that with the last girl.'

The last girl! Those three words hit Emily like a cold shower. They filled her head with questions. Who was the girl? Why was she sneaking around? And the scariest question of all – what happened to her? She looked at James, hoping to see some sympathy in his eyes, but there was none. He clenched his jaw and scowled. Confused and hurt she turned away. If they wanted to escape they'd have to trust one another. But from the expression on his face, trust between them seemed highly unlikely.

'You get a guard and that's all there is to it. Now where in the name of witchcraft is he? Spitfire,' she yelled, 'get over here.'

Scratching sounds from a cupboard were followed by a yowl so fierce that Emily fell back into her chair.

'Bat's blood,' muttered Ammonia. 'I forgot him. I locked him up after breakfast. He'll be in a filthy temper and he'll be ravenous. You'd better watch out or he'll have your fingers for supper.'

Emily hid her hands behind her back as the witch opened the cupboard door. A spitting, snarling bundle of fur flew out and launched itself at Ammonia.

'You brute,' yelled Ammonia. 'Get your claws out of my arm or I'll turn you into a beetle and stamp on you.'

The cat let go and dropped to the floor with a thud. 'Don't blame me,' it snarled. 'You're the one who made me mean and nasty.'

'I know,' said Ammonia, 'and I could do without your temper, but you've got to be fierce to keep these two in order. She nodded towards Emily and James. 'Save it for them.'

Spitfire glanced up. 'Not James Henry Watson. Why did you bring him back?'

'It's none of your business. Your job is to see he behaves himself, not to ask questions.'

As Spitfire prowled round James, the boy stuffed his hands inside his jumper and closed his eyes tightly.

Emily could see that he was shaking. I won't let the cat scare me, she said to herself. But when it stared at her with eyes that flashed green and amber, she found herself shaking almost as much as James. Even so, she forced herself to put on a brave face and stare back.

A low growl rumbled in the cat's throat as it walked round Emily's chair. 'It doesn't look very promising, but it can't be worse than the last one,' he said.

'How dare you call me 'it'? I'm a girl and my name is Emily. And how do you know whether I'm promising or not?'

Spitfire arched his back and spat.

Ammonia hooted with laughter. 'This is fun. A few sparks between you will keep you both on your toes. Mind you,' she said to Emily, 'Spitfire has the last word. If you step out of line he has my permission to show you how vicious he can be.'

'I can't wait,' growled Spitfire as he leapt onto the arm of Emily's chair.

'That's enough,' snapped Ammonia. 'Go on, get out. Catch something for your supper.' She raised her sleeve and pressed a button on a bracelet on her wrist. Instantly the cat disappeared. A few minutes later Ammonia pressed the button again and the cat returned.

He snarled, complaining that he hadn't had time to catch anything. 'I'm hungry,' he growled. 'It looks like fingers for supper after all.'

The witch laughed and threw him a biscuit. 'That'll have to do. Off you go to bed and don't let these two out of your sight.' She tossed a key to Emily. 'Get a good night's sleep,' she said. 'Tomorrow you start work in earnest.'

Chapter 19

Ammonia clicked her finger. Emily looked up as a strange whirring filled the air and a dark hole appeared in the ceiling. The sound grew louder as a spiral staircase came into view. Lower and lower it came, twisting and turning until it touched the floor next to Emily's chair.

'Up the spiralator,' said Ammonia, 'to the room with black bats on a yellow door. Don't touch any of the other doors or you'll get something you're not expecting.'

James stood up and walked onto the spiralator. Emily hesitated.

'Move yourself,' shouted Ammonia. 'Quick before it goes. If you miss it...'

Emily didn't wait to hear the alternative. She jumped onto the bottom step just as the spiralator began to turn. Spitfire, still sitting on the chair arm began to lick his paws.

Ammonia threw a book at him. 'You too,' she yelled.

With a huge leap Spitfire avoided the book and landed on the step beside Emily. Immediately the spiralator accelerated and whirled upwards. How far would it go? Emily had no idea. All she could see were the walls of a shaft. It was like being stuck in the lift, only this time they were moving. Up and up they went. Panic took over, another minute and she wouldn't be able to hold back her scream.

Just in time the spiralator slowed and clanked to a stop. Spitfire pushed his great head into the back of Emily's knees to force her off the step. James started walking along a corridor that stretched into the distance. He didn't look at the doors. He didn't look at Emily. He just walked with his head down. Spitfire followed, hurrying Emily along by spitting at her heels.

As Emily checked each yellow door, the patterns moved. Spiders scurried, cauldrons bubbled, and witches on broomsticks dodged one another as they flew. James stopped outside the yellow door with the pattern of flitting, fluttering bats.

Emily put the key in the keyhole, turned it and pushed the door open. James edged past her, wrapped himself in a blanket, curled up on one of the beds and turned his face to the wall. Emily tried to follow but Spitfire pushed her back.

'First things first,' he snarled. 'Lock the door and fasten the key to my collar.'

'No way.' Emily hung onto the key. 'I thought you'd sleep outside the door. I don't want to be locked in with you and I'm definitely not going to touch you.'

'Stop being stupid,' he growled. 'Ammonia's waiting. When the key clicks onto my collar it tells her that we're locked in for the night. That means she'll forget us and get on with her work.'

'And if I don't?'

'She'll come to sort us out.'

Was he speaking the truth? Emily wasn't sure. She didn't like the look of his huge mouth with its massive yellow teeth, or his enormous paws with their long, sharp claws. But she didn't like the sound of Ammonia coming to sort her out either.

James suddenly found his voice. It was a small voice, weak and shaky. 'Please do it. She'll eliminate us if you don't.'

The terror in his eyes convinced her that the matter was urgent. 'OK,' she said, but only if he keeps still and stops growling.'

Tentatively she edged towards the cat. His growl died away to a low rumble as he lifted up his chin. She poked the thick fur round his neck but she couldn't see a collar. 'How can I fasten it to your collar when you haven't got one?' she asked.

'It's there,' said Spitfire, 'under my fur. Feel for it, and get a move on.'

As she pushed her fingers into the matted lumps he spat and snarled. 'Be careful, that hurt.'

She dropped the key and backed away. The silence that followed was broken by a faint whirring sound.

'She's coming,' said Spitfire. 'Hurry. If you're quick she might turn back.'

James leapt off the bed, picked up the key and held it while Emily found the collar.

'How do I fasten it on?' she asked.

'There's a clip,' said James. 'Find it, quick.'

The sound of the spiralator grew louder. Emily's fingers ran round the collar, under Spitfire's chin and round the back of his neck. At last, just behind his right ear she found the clip. James handed her the key and she fastened it in place.

All three of them held their breath and listened. The sound was getting louder. James covered his ears. Emily's heart thumped so fast that she thought it would burst. Spitfire gave a little strangled cry. A great shudder ran through his body and in that moment something changed. Emily realised they were in this together. They might have disagreements between themselves but they were united in their fear of Ammonia.

For ten seconds the whirring continued. Then it stopped. When it started again it grew gradually fainter. They didn't speak. They didn't move until the sound died away completely. James collapsed on his bed and buried himself in his blanket.

Spitfire fell over on his side. 'Don't ever do that again,' he gasped. 'If she'd come in, it would have been the end for you. As for me, she'd have tightened my collar, and I'm half strangled as it is. The tiniest bit tighter and I won't be able to breathe at all.'

'I'm sorry,' Emily sobbed. 'I didn't know. I'm scared of Ammonia, but I'm scared of you as well. I didn't know she was worse than you.'

'Well I hope you know now. I could never be as bad as her. Now stop feeling sorry for yourself. You're stuck here until she's had enough of you. So you'd better get used to it.'

'But I don't want to get used to it. I want to go home.'

'Forget it,' he said. 'That's one thing that isn't going to happen.'

Emily looked at her watch. It was still showing 11.27. Her time hadn't moved. She threw herself on the bed and cried. She cried for her mum, her dad, her granny and grandpa. She cried for Great-gran, and she cried most of all because, according to Ammonia, no one knew that she was lost.

There was a thud as Spitfire leapt onto the bed beside her. He began to cough, harsh racking coughs that shook his body. He lifted up his paw and scratched at the collar. He coughed so much that Emily thought he would choke. Then he fell over, gasping for breath.

Despite her fear, Emily couldn't bear to see him in pain. She grabbed his collar and undid the buckle. Immediately, Spitfire stood up and arched his back. What happened next was so sudden and so unexpected that Emily could only watch in amazement. One second there was Spitfire with his huge head and matted fur. The next second there was a different cat – a handsome tabby with white paws. But before Emily had time to see it properly, it disappeared, and in its place stood a tall, bearded man.

Too shocked to speak, she cowered against the wall. This was magic of a different kind and she didn't know if it was good or bad. The man took her hands and smiled, and when he spoke his voice was deep and kind.

'Thank you, although thanks is a small word for the service you have done this night. Do not be afraid. I am here to help.'

'Who said that?' James pulled the blanket away from his face. He blinked and rubbed his eyes.

'It was Spitfire,' said Emily. 'He changed into a different cat and then into...' She looked up at the man. 'Who are you?'

'I cannot tell you,' he said, 'for if Ammonia hears my name we will be lost. Before we leave this room I will change back into Spitfire, and that is what you must call me. Even if I become a different cat, or take the form you see now, you must always call me Spitfire.'

James rubbed his eyes and looked from Emily to the man. His voice rose in panic. 'But how do we know you're not Ammonia in disguise? How do we know you're not trying to trick us?'

Chapter 20

As the man crossed the room James edged away to the farthest corner of the bed. 'Don't touch me. I don't trust you.' He pointed at Emily and glared. 'I don't trust you either. You said you wanted to be a witch. You're a spy. You're on Ammonia's side.'

'Don't be stupid,' said Emily. 'I was pretending. Ammonia said she'd send me home if I help her. So that's what I'm doing. Of course I don't want to be a witch. No one in their right mind would want to be a witch.' She shuddered at the thought. 'Imagine looking like Ammonia with her hideous finger and her disgusting warts.'

'You're the stupid one for believing her,' James retorted. 'She'll never let you go. She's a liar. She promised to let me go and then she turned me into a…' He paused as if it was too painful to speak the word. 'Next time she'll do it to you. I bet she doesn't know how to send people home. Why else would she keep everyone locked up in cages? If she knew how to let them go she'd do it, then she wouldn't have to bother feeding them.'

Emily was about to disagree when the man raised his hand. 'Children,' he said. 'Nothing is gained by quarrelling. We need to talk and we cannot afford to waste time.'

He crossed the room, put his ear to the door and listened. There were no footsteps in the corridor. There was no sound from the spiralator. Even the bats on the door had stopped their high-pitched chittering.

'I'm sure we're safe,' he said. 'If Ammonia knew you'd taken my collar off she'd be here by now. Please be silent. I must have a moment to contact my colleagues.'

He closed his eyes and placed his palms together as if he was praying. Emily looked at James. She raised her eyebrows and shrugged as if to ask how this strange man could contact anyone without a phone. James scowled and turned away. It was obvious that he still didn't trust her.

Eventually the man opened his eyes and began to speak. 'Listen carefully for I am about to reveal secrets of the utmost importance. They must never be mentioned outside this room. You must not think about them either because Ammonia can read your thoughts when she looks into your eyes. If I were to tell you everything it would take all night, but the crux of the matter is this. Ammonia has to sit an important exam. I do not know the details but I believe it is a matter of life and death.'

'Not exactly,' Emily interrupted. 'It's Exam 500, but that's only part of it. She has to make a spell that's never been made before. She has to perform it at a Festival and she needs a special costume that hasn't been made by magic. She brought me here to make it.'

She pointed to the array of brightly coloured flowers on her cardigan. 'Just because I embroidered this she thinks I can sew. The trouble is, this is all I can do, and I don't know what she'll do when I make a mess of it.'

'She'll turn you into a Devil's coach horse,' said James, 'and you'll have to eat worms and woodlice.'

Emily gasped, but before she could reply, the man reprimanded James. 'That is not at all helpful. There is no need to add to Emily's fear. We must be kind to one another and we must concentrate on Ammonia. What else can you tell me about her?'

Emily tried to recall everything Ammonia had said. 'She has to pass Exam 500 before they let her perform the spell. If her spell is the best one she'll join The Grand High Council of Malevolent Witches.'

'That is bad news indeed,' said the man. 'If a new witch joins The Council its power will double. There are twelve members now, and when they reach the magic number of thirteen, the Malevolent Witches will be so powerful that the Benevolent Wizards will struggle to counteract their evil magic.'

'But what's that got to do with you?' Emily asked. 'Unless you're a Benevolent Wizard.' She looked at the upturned curls on his shoes, past the sporran at his waist, on and up to his sparkling blue eyes. 'You're a wizard aren't you? That's why you can do magic.'

The wizard sighed. 'Yes, you are right, but now that you know, you must erase it from your minds, for if Ammonia suspects my true identity she will certainly eliminate me.'

James protested. 'Then you should eliminate her first.'

'As Spitfire I cannot do that, but in an extreme situation, if you were to remove my collar, it would be an option. However, it would defeat the reason for my being here. Ammonia is only one of many witches and I must wait for her to lead me to others. The Festival that Emily mentioned sounds like the perfect opportunity. It gives me hope and something to work towards, but I cannot succeed on my own. Can I rely on you two to help me?'

'I don't see what we can do,' said James.

'You can keep your ears and eyes open. You can find out about the spell she is working on. In her presence I must always be the cat known as Spitfire. That means wearing the collar. Unfortunately it stops me from communicating with other wizards. It also prevents me from knowing what is in Ammonia's mind. She will not think to hide her thoughts from two frightened children. The things you learn about her could make the difference between success and failure.'

James gave a half-hearted sort of laugh. 'What? Two kids and a cat! You must be joking.'

Angrily Emily turned on James. 'He's not just a cat. He's a wizard and he has a plan. We've got to help. It's our only chance of escaping.'

'Be patient, Emily,' said the wizard. 'James has had a terrifying experience. He is understandably pessimistic so we must make allowances for him.' He turned to James and added, 'but Emily is right. You must help. You are the only ones who can find out about her spell. If I know the nature of it I may be able to sabotage it. In my form as Spitfire, Ammonia has the upper hand, but I do not intend it always to be so. When we return to this room at night, you must remove my collar and I will change from cat to wizard. Then we can work on a plan together.'

'But,' said Emily, 'Ammonia said she had to compete against other witches. Any one of them could win the 13th place. What about them?'

'My colleagues are concerned with them,' he said. 'I am only required to deal with Ammonia. My chance to get into her stronghold came when the real Spitfire was outside the castle. Other wizards spirited him away and I turned myself into a cat that was identical in almost every way. The only difference was that I could use my power to send information back to my colleagues. At least that was the plan, but we had not bargained for the collar. It blocks my messages and stops me from thinking clearly.'

Emily picked up the collar and looked at it carefully. It was made of leather and there were sharp metal spikes on the inside. She winced at the thought of them sticking into Spitfire's neck. No wonder he was bad-tempered.

'If I have to put your collar back on,' she said, 'I'll keep it loose so it won't hurt so much.'

'That will be helpful,' said the wizard, 'but not so loose that Ammonia knows it has been tampered with. I dread to think what she will do if she suspects that we are friends.'

Chapter 21

'Now, we must sleep,' said the wizard. 'Ammonia may come for us at any time. It could be the middle of the night or halfway through the morning. Once she forgot for two days. I thought we'd starve to death.'

Emily's head filled with questions. 'You mean you and some other children? What happened to them? Where are they now?'

'They'll be in the cages,' said James. 'That's where they all end up.'

A picture of that awful smelly room flashed into Emily's mind. She shuddered as she recalled the scurrying sound of creatures hiding from Ammonia. 'I can't bear it, she said, 'tell me it isn't true.'

'I am sorry, I cannot do that,' said the wizard. 'It is true, and the more I think about it, the more I hope that James is right.'

'You can't mean that.' Emily almost exploded at the thought. 'Whose side are you really on?'

'Yours, of course,' said the wizard. 'Think about it. If the children are still here, whatever form they are in, we may be able to save them. If they have been eliminated we have lost our chance.'

'I don't think we stand a chance,' said James.

Emily considered their words then she looked at James. 'I know about Reverse Transformation because that's what she did to you. She tried it on a pig first, but something went wrong and it disappeared.'

'Eliminated,' said James.

'I don't think so,' said Emily. 'She said Reverse Transformation was a two part spell and if she missed the last part, the child would go home.'

The wizard had been listening intently. 'Tell me everything you can remember,' he said. 'The smallest detail may be of the greatest importance.'

'Well,' Emily began, 'she banged her walking stick. I can show you the mark on the floor where she hit it. Then a bookshelf slid away and there was a secret door. She turned the key three times and the door opened. The smell was awful. It nearly knocked me…'

'Not so fast,' said the wizard. 'Where does she keep the key?'

'Somewhere under her clothes, maybe in a pocket. I don't know exactly but it's on a key ring with lots of others, gold ones, silver ones, all shapes and sizes.'

'And the one she used, what was that like?'

'Silver and I think it was the biggest one.'

'An excellent start,' said the wizard. 'Do continue.'

'She sent me to find a bottle of green liquid. It took me ages. Oh! No!' Emily covered her mouth with her hands and looked at the wizard with worried eyes. 'We can't do it. We can't rescue anyone. There was only one bottle and we used most of it on the pig. Then we used the rest on James so there's only a tiny drop left. She won't make any more because she's got me and James and she won't need any more helpers. Unless one of us misbehaves…'

'Don't look at me,' James backed away in horror. 'I'm not going to misbehave so she'll make more.'

'I wouldn't expect you to,' said Emily, 'maybe…'

'Please keep to the point,' said the wizard. 'You are confusing me. What happened when you returned with the green bottle?'

'She chose the most enormous pig. Its name was Joanna something. Ammonia said she'd eaten the chocolate off the top of a cake…'

'I remember her,' James cut in. 'She never stopped eating. That's why Ammonia transformed her. I can't remember her surname but I don't suppose it matters.'

'It does matter,' said Emily.' I want to know what happened.' She turned to the wizard. 'If she went home her time will have started again and no-one will have missed her. But if she's been eliminated she'll have disappeared.'

The wizard raised his eyebrows. 'Can you be sure?'

'Not absolutely,' said Emily. 'But that's what Ammonia told me. And if Joanna has disappeared her parents will call the police. She'll be in the papers and on TV. Everyone will know about her.'

James frowned. 'I don't get it. I was her helper and she never told me anything. I think you're on her side.'

'Well I'm not.' Emily thumped the bedside table. 'I never heard anything so ridiculous. She put a spell on me. She made me talk. She said we had to be friends. So I pretended. I talked to her, but I watched and listened too. And all the time I was trying to find a way to escape.'

'You did well,' said the wizard, 'but let's get back to Joanna. What did Ammonia do to her?'

'She sprayed her with green liquid and it turned into foam, then it exploded and she disappeared.'

'Well, that's not what happened to me,' said James, 'because I'm still here.'

'That's because Ammonia did the second part of the spell. She shouted 'cut' at the same time as the explosion. She didn't do it for Joanna because she fell over and missed the right moment.'

James looked thoughtful. 'I suppose that was lucky for me,' he said. 'If she'd kept Joanna she wouldn't have needed me. I'd still be a …a…'

'Slug,' said Emily. She looked at his pale face and instantly regretted saying the hated word. 'I'm sorry. I shouldn't have reminded you.'

'No, you should not,' said the wizard, 'although it is useful for me to know.' He stroked his beard and nodded thoughtfully. 'I begin to understand. If the green potion sent Joanna home we may be able to use it on the other children. I don't know when we will get a chance, but we must be prepared. You must persuade her to make some more.'

'And I must make her costume for the Festival,' said Emily.

'What about me?' James asked.

'Sorry,' said Emily. 'She brought you back to do the housework. Look on the bright side though, washing up is better than being a...a you know what.'

James groaned. 'Just my rotten luck,' he said. 'I hate washing-up and there's mountains of it. I'd better get some rest.'

Emily was ready to do the same but the wizard was still sitting on her bed. 'We need another bed,' she said. 'Ammonia never guessed there'd be three of us.'

'Don't worry about me,' said the wizard. 'I would dearly love to spend a night in my own skin but it cannot be. I must change into Spitfire in case she comes to let us out.'

'But we've got a key. Why don't we let ourselves out?'

115

'If only it were that easy,' he sighed, 'but we cannot unlock the door from the inside. She is afraid that we will find a means of escape. Now, try to sleep. Tomorrow night we will continue with our plans.'

Emily had so many thoughts running through her head that she thought she'd never sleep. By the dim light of the bedside lamp she watched him put the wand back in his sleeve. Instantly he disappeared and in his place stood a handsome tabby cat. It picked up the collar in its mouth, padded across the bed and dropped it in front of her.

'As soon as I turn into Spitfire you must fasten the collar,' he whispered. 'We must be ready for Ammonia's return.'

Before she had time to answer, Spitfire stood over her. A low growl started in his throat. His eyes glowed green in the half-light. Saliva dripped from his yellow teeth. He struggled against her, tossing his head and backing away from the collar.

She forced the collar over his neck and had almost fastened the buckle when he wriggled out of her grasp. All she had to do was thread the end of the collar through the loop, but he seemed determined to stop her. He leapt off the bed and prowled round the room. Every time she drew close he spat and lashed out with his claws. Still she refused to give up. Whatever he did to her, she had to finish fastening the collar. If Ammonia noticed that it had been tampered with, it would be the end for all of them.

Chapter 22

For Emily, the night passed slowly. Spitfire remained curled up on her bed and the slightest movement made him growl. The scratches from his claws were stinging. They criss-crossed her face and arms as well as her hands. She lay, rigid with fear, half-expecting him to pounce and tear her to shreds. She had dozed a little but was awake when the spiralator hummed and clanked to a stop.

Spitfire nudged her with his great head. 'Get up, get a move on, she's coming.' Then he leapt across to James's bed and repeated the message.

Emily yawned. James, still clutching his blanket, struggled to his feet. The sound of Ammonia's footsteps drew closer. Emily sat on the edge of the bed. She rubbed her eyes and winced as she touched the scratches on her cheeks.

Spitfire arched his back. 'Pull yourselves together,' he spat. 'Look lively or she'll have your guts for garters.'

The door opened and there stood the witch. 'Rise and shine,' she cackled. 'Aren't I the lucky one, two helpers today. Come along, there's work to be done.' She caught hold of James's blanket and tugged it so hard that he almost fell over. She grabbed Emily by the shoulder and pulled her to her feet.

'Well, well,' she said as she caught sight of the scratches. 'What have we here?' She glanced at Spitfire. 'So, you two had an argument. What was it about?'

Before Spitfire could tell the truth, Emily blurted out an explanation. She hung her head so that Ammonia couldn't look into her eyes. 'I wanted to

117

escape. I tried to steal the key, but he wouldn't let me and I got scratched. I'm sorry, I know it was stupid and I promise I won't do it again.'

The witch narrowed her eyes as she turned to James. 'Is that the truth?'

Emily held her breath, terrified that James would contradict her.

'I don't know,' he mumbled. 'I went to sleep. I didn't see anything.'

To Emily's relief, Ammonia didn't ask any more questions, and once they were downstairs, Spitfire was sent outside. The witch dished out three bowls of porridge and told them to hurry up and eat it. They ate quickly, but Ammonia took her time. After a few mouthfuls she turned her attention to James.

'Look at me and listen because I'll only say this once.'

Emily glanced at James. He was gripping his spoon so tightly that his knuckles were white. She reached under the table, put her hand on his knee and squeezed. For a moment he looked startled, but he managed to raise his eyes to the witch.

'You,' she said, 'are head housekeeper. Do you know what that means?'

James looked uncertain. 'I think so, but...'

'Perhaps you'd better remind him,' said Emily. 'Then there won't be any confusion.'

'Good thinking,' said the witch as she reached across the table and gripped James by the chin. 'It means cooking. Soups and stews will do at a pinch, although cakes and puddings wouldn't come amiss. If there's anything you need just think about it, and it'll be there in the cupboard. But cooking isn't all. It means cleaning, washing, tidying and seeing to the fire. It means anything and everything that needs doing. Use your initiative, keep yourself busy, run the house like clockwork and I won't interfere. If you let things slide you know what'll happen, don't you?'

James tried to nod but the grip on his chin stopped him from moving. 'Yes,' he whispered, 'but I'm sorry. I...I don't know how to cook.'

'Not as sorry as you will be,' snapped the witch. 'I'll have to find someone else. This seems to be the ideal time for elimin...'

'No,' shouted Emily, 'that's...' She stopped and lowered her voice. 'I mean, please don't. Let me help with the cooking. It'll be a change from sewing. Besides, you used the last of the green spray so you can't do a Reverse Transformation until you make some more.'

'Bother!' Ammonia muttered. 'I was looking forward to demonstrating my Elimination Spell. It's fun and you haven't seen it yet.'

'I have seen it,' said Emily, 'I saw you eliminate the bluebottle, and didn't you eliminate that big fat pig?'

'Joanna Blackstock? No,' said Ammonia. 'That wasn't elimination. It was supposed to be Reverse Transformation, but I sent her home by mistake. Forget her. It's James we have to consider.' She grinned at Emily. 'I think we should do something to him. It's time for a laugh. Any ideas?'

Emily's mind was racing. Joanna had gone home. If they could persuade Ammonia to make more potion, and if she could get into Ammonia's frightful zoo, she could release everyone. She pushed the thoughts away and looked at James. He'd been clearing the table when

119

Ammonia mentioned elimination, but he'd stopped as if he was playing Statues. One leg was resting on the tip of his toe. In one hand was a spoon and the other held a porridge bowl. The spoon was shaking and she daren't think what would happen if he dropped the bowl. Although they hadn't made friends, although he still regarded her with suspicion, she couldn't stand back while Ammonia eliminated him.

'I don't see why you need to do anything,' she said. 'If he doesn't clean up every day we'll never get the place tidy. Please let me help him to cook. I'll still have time to sew, I promise. And if you do eliminate him you'll have to find someone to take his place.'

Ammonia twitched her nose and fiddled with the hairs on the end of her wart. 'Maybe, you're right,' she said. 'I'll give him one more chance. Think yourself lucky, James Henry Watson. You have Emily to thank for saving you this time.'

Carefully, very carefully, James placed his foot firmly on the floor. He took the last few steps to the sink. From across the room, Emily heard his sigh of relief as he put down the bowl.

Ammonia turned to Emily. 'I have things to do,' she said, 'and Spitfire's out hunting so you can help James to tidy up. We can talk about sewing later.'

For the next hour Ammonia pored over a book while the two children slaved in the kitchen. When the washing up was done they stood side-by-side, chopping potatoes, carrots, onions and leeks. Emily added lentils and soon her favourite soup was bubbling away on the hob. At least, if she did the cooking, the food would be worth eating. Neither of them dared utter a word, but once, Emily caught

James's eye. She gave him a ghost of a smile. He didn't smile back but he no longer scowled at her.

The soup was a success, and as soon as they'd finished, Ammonia pressed the button on her bracelet. Spitfire came hurtling back, licking his mouth as if he'd had a good meal, then he turned around on the sofa and settled down to sleep. Ammonia leapt to her feet, crossed the room and poked him with her stick.

'Wake up, you lazy brute,' she ordered. 'I'm going upstairs and you're on guard.'

Spitfire opened one eye then closed it. Ammonia poked him again. He grabbed the stick in his teeth, tossed his head and tried to wrench it from her grasp.

'Drop it,' she shouted, 'do as I say or I'll tighten your collar.'

The cat dropped the stick and stood up. He arched his back and stretched. 'All right,' he snarled. 'I heard you. I'm on guard and they'd better behave themselves.'

Chapter 23

With a swift backward glance Ammonia disappeared up the spiralator. Emily put her hand on James's shoulder.

'Try not to worry,' she said. 'We'll…'

Spitfire was across the room in a moment. He leapt onto the draining board and snarled. 'You'll do what?'

Emily dodged away from the reach of his claws. How was it possible? How could a kind, gentle wizard be locked inside this vicious monster of a cat?

He snarled again. 'Tell me or I'll make you tell me.'

Emily folded her arms and scowled. 'I was going to say that we'll do as we're told and then Ammonia won't do anything horrible to us. And you,' she unfolded her arms and pointed her finger at him, 'won't need to scratch me again.'

The cat spat. 'Don't be too sure about that. Put a foot wrong and I'll do more than scratch.'

Emily sighed. 'Aren't you tired of being bad-tempered? We can't escape so why don't you get out of our way? And get off the draining board? It's unhygienic.'

The cat ignored her. He turned his back, licked his paws and began to wash his face.

'I told you to move,' Emily repeated.

Very slowly, Spitfire washed behind his ears. When he'd finished, he spat in Emily's direction. 'All right I'll move, but you put a foot wrong and…'

'I know. You'll do more than scratch,' Emily retorted, 'but why don't you try being nice for a change?'

James had stood, open-mouthed throughout their conversation. 'I don't know how you dare talk back to him,' he said. 'He scares me stiff, and I'm worried. There's nothing else to do and if I stop working ...' His voice tailed away to a whimper.

'Then don't stop.' Emily snapped. 'You've got to be brave. The place is filthy. It's a wonder we don't die from a disgusting tummy bug. Everything needs a good scrub. Empty the cupboards. Clean the shelves. It doesn't matter if you do the same things over and over again. As long as you keep working she'll leave you alone. Just get on with it. I have to make Ammonia's costume. Now that really is something to worry about.'

She picked up the sketchbook and sat at the table. Spitfire leapt up next to her. He made it impossible for her to concentrate. She stared back, trying to break through the magic that bound him, trying to reach the wizard beneath his disguise. Tentatively she reached out, but the cat was too quick for her. His paw flashed out and added another scratch to the ones he'd inflicted the night before.

'Ouch!' She pulled her hand back. 'You didn't have to do that.'

But maybe he did. Maybe that's how Ammonia had programmed him. Maybe he had no free will at all. One thing was certain. He'd forgotten everything that had happened in the bedroom. He probably didn't even know that he was a wizard. Perhaps that was for the best. If Ammonia sensed a change in him they would all be in danger. But what would happen when they were locked away for the night? How could she remove his collar, and more importantly, how could she put it back on?

She moved to a chair by the fire but Spitfire followed. She turned away from him and started to draw. She sketched dresses, cloaks and hats but none of them looked spectacular. She drew in silence, and all the while James busied himself, sweeping ashes from the hearth and scrubbing the floor.

After working for half an hour Emily automatically looked at her watch. Nothing had changed. It still showed 11.27. Tears welled up when she thought of Mum waiting in the supermarket café, hot chocolate and a cinnamon bagel on the table. What would happen? Would the hot chocolate go cold? Would the bagel go stale? If Ammonia had spoken the truth, neither of these things would happen. When she got back, if she got back, she would eat and drink and start her life again as if nothing had happened. But would the horrible memories stay in her head, giving her bad dreams, making her afraid to let her mum out of her sight?

The spiralator whirred. It clanked to a stop and the witch appeared, half-hidden under armfuls of clothes. On the step beside her was a box, and on the step above stood a huge wicker basket.

'Don't just stand there,' she shouted. 'Come here and help.'

She dumped the clothes on a chair while James grabbed the box and Emily dragged the basket into a space on the floor.

'Sort through those,' she said, 'and James can help. They're my mother's clothes. You can cut them up, do anything you like, as long as you turn them into a fabulous costume.'

Emily put a stool in the middle of the floor. 'Stand on that,' she said to James, 'and hold them up so I can see them properly.'

There was a black velvet cloak and a cloak of sparkly silver fabric. There were dresses of every imaginable colour. There were dresses with short sleeves, dresses with long sleeves and dresses with no sleeves at all. There were dresses with gathered skirts and dresses with pleats. There were dozens of dresses but when James held up the last one she shook her head in despair.

'What now?' James asked.

'I don't know. The cloak will be fine I'll use the black one and line it with the silver one, but I'm not sure about the dress. I'll have to use one of them and then I'll have to decorate it. Ammonia wants embroidery but it won't show up on the stage. It needs something brighter and bolder.'

'I wonder.' James stopped as if he was afraid to suggest anything.

'If you have an idea, please tell me,' said Emily, 'because I can't think of anything.'

'Well, my mum made a chicken costume for my little sister. You could…'

'No I couldn't. I can't turn Ammonia into a chicken.'

'I know that,' James retorted. 'Just listen. It's the way she did it that might help. We cut shapes out of crepe paper, and then we tacked them to a leotard until it was hidden under yellow paper feathers.'

Emily's face almost broke into a smile. Suddenly she could see the finished costume. It would fall in smooth lines from shoulder to floor. There would be a long train and sleeves that widened at the wrist. It would be covered with hundreds of coloured scraps and it would look fantastic.

'I've got it,' she cried. 'Thanks, James. I've seen the very one.' She sorted through the dresses again and held up the pink one. 'This is it. It's the perfect shape.'

'What are you talking about?' Ammonia demanded.

'About your costume,' said Emily. 'I know what I want to do but it's too much work for me on my own. Can James help me?' She looked hopefully at the witch.

Ammonia shrugged. 'As long as it doesn't interfere with his other work, but let me see what you have in mind.'

Emily held up the pink dress, but before she could start to explain Ammonia turned red with fury.

'Pink,' she yelled as she stamped her feet. 'Pink,' she shrieked as she stormed across the room. 'Pink,' she screamed as she snatched the dress from Emily's hand. 'Pink! I won't be seen dead in pink. Pink is for babies. Pink is for fairies. Pink was for wimps like my mother. Don't you dare expect me to wear pink.'

She threw the offending dress across the room and kicked the other clothes aside. 'You, my girl, will have to think again.'

Chapter 24

James scurried to pick up the scattered clothes. He placed them carefully across a chair while Emily tried to think of an alternative. She sorted through the box and the basket. She found lace and ribbons, beads and buttons and all kinds of sparkly things. They would be useful but her mind was still fixed on the pink dress. Determined to change Ammonia's mind she carried it across to her.

As soon as the witch saw it, she flew into another rage. 'Show me that again,' she screeched, 'and I'll tear it to shreds. I will not have pink.'

Emily backed away, but she refused to give in. She whispered instructions to James. 'Cut the skirts off the other dresses. I don't care what she says. I'm using the pink one. It's the only suitable style and the pink won't show when I've finished with it.'

James grabbed her arm. 'Don't. She'll be furious. Please don't.'

Emily ignored him. 'I've got to use it. None of the others will do. When it's finished she'll thank me, you'll see.'

She sat down to draw and twenty minutes later she took the sketch to Ammonia. 'There'll be hundreds of little pieces and they'll stick out like petals,' she explained.

'Petals!' Ammonia snorted. 'Don't you dare turn me into a flower.'

'I won't,' said Emily. 'We'll use squares. They'll ripple and swirl when you turn round.' She held out the sketch. 'What do you think?'

127

Ammonia snatched it. 'Boring,' she said with a snort, 'dark and boring. The shape's fine but I don't want dark colours. I want red and orange and yellow. I want green and turquoise and gold. I want silver and bright blue and purple. I want every colour you can find. I want them all mixed up together. I want a dress as bright as a rainbow, but I will not have pink. And where's the embroidery? I must have embroidery.'

Emily hesitated. 'Embroidery won't work. When you're up on the stage the audience won't be able to see it. Look, I'll show you.' She put on Great-gran's cardigan, walked to the far end of the room and looked over her shoulder at Ammonia. 'I bet you can't tell what the patterns are. I bet you can't even see them.'

'I don't care.' Ammonia stamped her foot. 'I've set my heart on embroidery and embroidery I will have.'

'Please think again,' said Emily. 'What's the point of embroidering for hours if no-one can see it?' She sighed and thought for a moment.' If I use really thick wool it might work on the cloak, but not on the dress. The trouble is we haven't got any wool. You'll have to go shopping if you want embroidery.'

'There's no time for shopping,' Ammonia snapped. 'You'll have to think of something. I want embroidery. I want all the colours but I will not have pink.'

Emily started to protest, but when Ammonia lifted her hideous finger, she hurried back to James. He'd put the pink dress on one side and was cutting the skirts from the other dresses. He didn't look up. Emily threaded her needle and set to work on the cloak, but even as she sewed, she watched and listened, hoping to discover the secret of Ammonia's special spell.

The afternoon passed slowly. James began to cut squares from the dresses. Apart from the snip of scissors, few sounds came to break the tense, unpleasant silence. Once or twice Ammonia muttered as she worked. Every now and then, James sniffed to hold back his tears. He shivered a great deal as if he was cold, but Emily knew that it was caused by fear. Ammonia yawned, stretched and slipped her hand inside the neck of her dress.

Emily watched. She re-arranged her hair so that it fell like a curtain across her face. She peered through it and saw that Ammonia was holding the locket that she'd held the day before. She was opening it, grinning to herself, taking something out, stretching it between her fingers. She was mumbling, and among the words she uttered was the word that Emily didn't understand – retribution. Once again, Ammonia wound the invisible thing around her finger. The firelight flickered, and for the split of a second Emily caught a glint of silver.

What could it be? What did people keep in lockets? Wasn't it usually photographs and locks of hair? Hair. That was it. Not a curl of hair held in a ribbon, but a single hair, an extremely long, silver hair. It was a clue to Ammonia's spell. It had to be. Her heart pounded. She was bursting to tell James. She was bursting to tell the wizard, but she daren't breathe a word until all three of them were safely inside the bedroom.

James was still snipping away with his scissors. The pile of coloured squares was growing. Emily left the cloak. She took the squares and began to stitch them to the dress. She started at the hem of the sleeve, overlapping the squares so that the pink fabric was hidden. Pushing the needle through was hard, but she went on sewing until her fingers ached. Then she paused to see how much she'd done. Only three rows were finished, but already the pattern was forming. Maybe Ammonia was right after all. The crazy mix of colours looked amazing, but there were many metres to cover. At this rate she would be sewing forever.

'Don't cut any more small squares,' she said to James. 'Big ones will look better on the skirt and they'll be quicker to sew.' She took the scissors from him and cut a ten centimetre square. 'There, lets have lots of those.'

The witch's, harsh voice called across the room. 'You're talking again and why aren't you making supper? You've ten minutes to get it on the table and if it isn't, I'll be thinking devil's coach horses.'

James gasped. His hand shook so much that his scissors dropped to the floor with a clatter. Emily flew into a panic. Her thoughts raced. What did Mum cook when they were in a hurry? She steadied herself and answered as calmly as she could. 'It's cheese omelette and salad. It doesn't take long. We're just about to start.'

Ammonia seemed satisfied. James hurried to the kitchen. Emily hid her work at the bottom of the wicker basket. Ammonia would have to see it eventually, but the longer it remained a secret the better it would be. She had to prove that she could hide every trace of pink. It was too late to change direction now. All the other dresses had been cut.

Supper was ready with barely a second to spare. Ammonia made no comment. She forked the food into her mouth with one hand and scribbled in a book with the other. Emily tried to see what she was writing, but it looked like a complicated maths problem – a mixture of letters and numbers that she couldn't understand at all.

A sudden, strident beeping filled the room. It came from the television and it startled them all. Emily stuck her fingers in her ears. James covered his ears too. Spitfire woke up and yowled in protest. Ammonia leapt to her feet and rushed to the television set. She turned knobs and pressed buttons until the beeping stopped and crackling sounds took over. Wavy lines moved across the screen like crazy lightning. She cursed and thumped the top of the set with her fist.

'Come on,' she urged as she thumped it again. The wavy lines slowed and stopped. A single word appeared on the screen, a word in black writing on a blood red background – WITCHVISION.

'Scram,' she shouted to James and Emily. 'Get to bed. This isn't for the likes of you.' She swung her stick at Spitfire and caught him across the side of his head. 'Get up you good-for-nothing brute. Up the spiralator and don't let me hear a peep out of you until morning.'

Chapter 25

Emily left the table and looked round, but the spiralator was nowhere to be seen. 'We can't go,' she called. 'You haven't sent for it.'

Ammonia didn't hear, for at that moment, a fanfare of trumpets sounded. Spitfire curled up and went back to sleep. Emily was about to call Ammonia again when the trumpets stopped and a voice took over.

'Calling all Malevolent Witches. The news today contains a matter of extreme urgency. Our newsreader is Vitriola Sniff. Listen carefully to what she has to say.'

This was far too interesting to miss. Emily didn't call Ammonia again. Instead she listened, hoping to learn something important. After all, it wasn't her fault that Ammonia had forgotten to send for the spiralator. She turned her attention to the television and gasped at the sight of another ghastly witch.

Apart from the fact that she was skinny, Vitriola Sniff was nothing like Ammonia.

Her grey hair was a frizz of curls and she was so small that only her head and shoulders showed above the news desk. She blew her long hooked nose, cleared her throat and began to speak in a high, piping voice.

'Copies of the answers to Exam 500 have been stolen. The culprit or culprits, when they are found, will receive the ultimate punishment.'

A second witch elbowed Vitriola out of the way. 'Cheats will not be allowed to live,' she screeched. 'They'll be stripped of their warts, they will forfeit their spells and be publicly eliminated.'

132

Vitriola drew herself up to her full height. It didn't impress anyone for she didn't even reach the other witch's shoulder. 'Mandragora Twitch,' she squeaked. 'Get out of my way. I must finish the news. The exam paper has been changed, and to avoid further cheating, Exam 500 will take place tomorrow.'

There was sudden uproar. The camera panned across the live audience. Witches shook their fists and shouted. They drummed their feet and hissed their disapproval.

The sight of so many witches hit Emily like a punch. Even in her worst nightmares she couldn't have imagined so many.

'Order,' called Vitriola. 'I must have order.' Her voice was so weak that not a single witch responded.

Mandragora roared at the top of her voice. 'Silence. You must hear the rest of the announcement.'

The witches gradually settled down. Mandragora snatched the sheaf of papers from Vitriola's hand. 'Call yourself a newsreader,' she sneered. 'I'll show you how it's done.' She adjusted her glasses and began to read. 'We are aware that there will be complaints, but The Grand High Council has made its decision and there is no appeal. Entrants must attend the usual venue at six o'clock in the morning. Any witch who fails to arrive by that time will be disqualified.' She slammed the papers onto the desk and her voice rose. 'Eliminate the cheats,' she bellowed. 'Eliminate the cheats.'

Vitriola hopped up and down and shook her fists at Mandragora. The camera moved in for a close-up. Her face was white and her assorted warts stood out, red and angry. 'Don't think you can make a fool of me,' she shrieked. 'Just because you're bigger than me doesn't mean you're better. I'm twice as good a witch as you. Just you wait for the Festival and I'll prove it.'

Mandragora laughed. 'Don't forget you have to pass the exam first. I doubt if you'll manage, but even if you do, my spell will beat yours.'

The television crackled and sparked. The picture tore into shreds and the screen went black. Emily expected Ammonia to lose her temper about the changed date, but she did no such thing. She laughed uproariously, picked up her skirts and danced.

'Twitch and Sniff! What a feeble pair. As for witches stealing answers. How stupid is that?'

She stopped in the middle of her dance and glared at Emily and James. 'Why are you still here? I sent you to bed?'

'You forgot the spiralator,' Emily explained. 'We tried to tell you but you wouldn't listen. Then the witch said her message was important and we daren't interrupt in case you missed it.'

'For once you did the right thing,' said Ammonia. 'Mind you, if you'd heard a Top Secret Broadcast it would have meant elimination for you both.'

Emily grabbed the chair to steady herself as she realised the enormity of the risk she'd taken.

'Don't worry,' Ammonia continued, 'As it is, we can celebrate. Chocolate biscuits all round.'

Emily raised her eyebrows. 'What is there to celebrate?'

'Plenty. The exam is tomorrow and I'm ready for it.' Ammonia caught Emily by one hand and James by the other. She whirled them round the room until they were dizzy. Eventually she let them go, threw herself into a chair and roared with laughter.

'I don't see what's funny,' said Emily. 'You can't be sure you'll pass unless you're going to cheat.'

'Of course I'm going to cheat. Any witch worthy of being a witch has to cheat. It's the only way. The trick is to avoid getting caught. If they're too stupid to notice it's their fault, not mine. I perfected the art of cheating when I sat Exam 100. I used the same method for Exams 200, 300 and 400 and still they didn't work out how I did it. There's no reason why it shouldn't work again. Anyway, I can't play fair. I'm sure I'd fail and then I wouldn't be allowed to perform my spell. It's the most daring spell that's ever been seen. It will secure the future of Malevolent Witchery. It'll prove that I deserve the thirteenth chair. It'll be the final downfall of the Ben...' She clapped her hand over her mouth and stopped in the middle of a word.

Emily's mind raced. She guessed what Ammonia was going to say and the sooner she told the wizard, the better.

'Now,' said Ammonia. 'I must prepare for tomorrow. Take your biscuits to bed and off you go. Spitfire will make sure you don't get up to mischief while I'm gone and you both work on my costume.'

The prospect of several hours without Ammonia filled Emily with hope. She struggled to stop her excitement bubbling over. She avoided Ammonia's eyes and forced herself to think about practical things.

'I hope you can go shopping while you're away,' she said. 'If you still want me to embroider, I'll need lots of thick wool. I also need a bottle of fabric glue and half a dozen glue brushes.'

'You don't want much then.' Ammonia's tone bristled with sarcasm. 'What if I haven't time? What then?'

Emily shrugged. 'It's up to you. If you don't bring the things I've asked for, I won't be able to finish the costume.'

Ammonia whipped round and caught her by the chin. She looked deep into Emily's eyes, but Emily was ready. Over and over in her head she repeated the words. I can't embroider without wool and I can't finish the dress without fabric glue.

'Oh!' she added out loud. 'I'll need some special needles, ones with very sharp points and very big eyes. I won't be able to embroider the cloak without them.'

Ammonia let go of Emily's chin. 'I'll bring what I can, and you'll have to make the best of it. Now where's that dratted cat. Spitfire, get to bed and mind there's no nonsense tonight.'

Spitfire leapt to his feet as the spiralator descended. He snarled and spat until Emily and James stepped aboard. Up they went, whirring and clanking. As they rose higher and higher, Emily pondered on all the things she'd heard. The witches who failed the exam would be eliminated, and Ammonia would be eliminated if they caught her cheating.

Emily smiled at the thought, but her smile froze as she wondered what would happen if Ammonia didn't return. They had no green potion to release the other children. They had no way out of the fortress. Did that mean they'd be trapped forever?

Chapter 26

Emily remembered the events of the previous night. She locked the door and approached Spitfire with the key. He stood still while she clipped it onto his collar, but as soon as she touched the buckle he jerked away and batted her with his paw.

'Come on,' she coaxed. 'Let me take it off.'

He backed away, baring his yellow teeth and arching his back.

'Let her take it off,' said James, 'you'll feel better.'

'Don't be stupid.' Spitfire leapt onto James's bed and spat. 'Ammonia would know. She'd rush up here with an even worse punishment. I daren't take the risk.' He turned his back on James, curled up at the bottom of the bed and closed his eyes.

Emily twisted her fingers together. She frowned and sighed and paced up and down. She had to tell the wizard about all the things she'd heard. It wasn't just important. It was vital. She hesitated as she looked at the red scratches on her hands.

'I don't care if he scratches me to pieces,' she said. 'I've got to take it off.'

'No,' said James. 'It's my turn. Let me try.' Very slowly he edged down the bed and reached for the collar, but Spitfire was too quick for him. He lashed out with his claws and James fell back with beads of blood forming on his arm.

Emily expected James to cry out. She expected him to give up because, so far, he'd been a bit of a wimp. But she was wrong. He was angry.

'You stupid animal,' he shouted. 'We're trying to help. Why can't you get it into your thick head?'

'Don't shout at me,' Spitfire snarled. 'I can't let you take it off. It's more than my life's worth.'

'That's not what you said last night,' said James. 'You'd have choked if Emily hadn't taken it off. You were gasping for breath and Ammonia didn't find out. Let me take it off. We'll put it back on before morning.'

Spitfire shook his great head. 'I don't know what you're talking about and I don't know why you care anyway. You've no reason to be nice to me. You're trying to trick me and I don't know why.'

'Because you're not really Spitfire,' said Emily. 'Ammonia's put a spell on you. The collar is part of it.'

'Don't make me laugh,' said the cat. 'You think you can steal the key. You think you can escape, but you can't. It's impossible. No-one has ever escaped and no-one ever will. Now do as I say and leave me alone.'

'Forget it,' said Emily. 'Let him sleep.'

'But,' James protested. 'We've got to…'

'I said forget it, 'Emily insisted. 'Why should we care if he's uncomfortable? Why should we care if Ammonia has him under a spell.' She put her finger to her lips and winked.

Spitfire was soon asleep. His breathing slowed and he began to snore. Emily picked up her pillow. Afraid of waking him, she mimed what she intended to do. She pointed to herself, lifted the pillow and pointed to Spitfire. Then she pointed to James and mimed the action of removing the collar.

James nodded. Slowly, they got to their feet and tiptoed towards the sleeping cat. Emily raised the pillow, brought it swiftly down on Spitfire's body and threw herself on top. The cat was trapped. His paws were hidden under his body. He spat and snarled and struggled to free himself, but Emily held him fast. James caught hold of the collar and managed to undo the buckle.

'Yes!' Emily lifted the pillow and stepped back.

As the collar fell away Spitfire shook himself and changed into the handsome tabby cat. A second later he was transformed into the wizard.

'Emily, James.' He took hold of their hands, frowned at the array of scratches and apologized for causing them pain.

'It wasn't your fault,' said James, 'but we must have an easier way of taking your collar off.'

'And putting it back on,' Emily added, 'but let's talk about that later. I must tell you about the Witchvision broadcast. There were two witches and they're both planning to perform at the Festival.'

'Excellent,' said the wizard. 'Can you describe them?'

'One was small and skinny with frizzy hair and the other was big and bossy. One was called Snip or...'

'Sniff,' suggested the wizard.

'Yes,' said James, 'and the other was Twitch.'

'Members of two powerful clans,' said the wizard, but can you remember their first names?'

James and Emily had to admit that they couldn't.

'In that case, you must close your eyes and open your ears to the memory.'

As soon as they closed their eyes, the strangest thing happened. James began to speak. 'Our newsreader is Vitriola Sniff. Listen carefully to what she has to say.'

Emily took over.' Copies of the answers to Exam 500 have been stolen. The culprit or culprits, when they are found, will receive the ultimate punishment.'

'Cheats will not be allowed to live,' added James. 'They will be stripped of their warts, they will forfeit their spells and be publicly eliminated.'

Emily spoke again. 'Mandragora Twitch, get out of my way. I must finish the news. The exam paper has been changed, and to avoid further cheating, Exam 500 will take place tomorrow.'

'Order.' said Emily. 'I must have order.'

'Silence,' called James. 'We must hear the rest. Call yourself a newsreader. I'll show you how it's done. We are aware that honest witches will complain, but The Grand High Council has made its decision and there is no appeal. Entrants must attend the usual venue at six o'clock in the morning. Any witch who fails to arrive by that time will be disqualified. Eliminate the cheats. Eliminate the cheats.'

'Don't think you can make a fool of me,' said Emily. 'Just because you're bigger than me doesn't mean you're better. I'm twice as good a witch as you. Just you wait for the Festival and I'll prove it.'

James laughed. 'Don't forget you have to pass the exam first. I doubt if you'll manage, but even if you do, my spell will beat yours.'

James was still laughing when he opened his eyes. 'What's funny,' he asked. 'Why am I laughing? And what happened? I feel really odd as if someone was filling my head with angry words.'

'Me too,' said Emily, 'but I wasn't laughing. I felt really nervous.'

'That does not surprise me,' said the wizard. 'Vitriola Sniff is inferior to Mandragora Twitch, and she knows it, although she pretends otherwise.'

He put his hand on James's shoulder. 'I'm sorry that you found that disturbing. I made you repeat everything that you had heard because I had to know the details. You spoke Mandragora's words and you laughed because she laughed.'

'Well, I hope you don't make me do it again,' said James. 'I felt really mean.'

The wizard was silent for a moment. Then he said, 'I have transmitted the information to my colleagues. They will put Vitriola and Mandragora under surveillance. Now what can you tell me about Ammonia's plans?'

'She's going to sit Exam 500 tomorrow and she's going to cheat,' said Emily. 'Can't we stop her?'

'Why don't you get someone to follow her to the exam?' James asked. 'Wouldn't that be helpful?'

'It would,' said the wizard. 'I shall arrange it.'

Emily waited while he contacted his colleagues, and then she asked how to replace his collar without getting scratched.

'Put it on the tabby cat,' he said.

'It might work,' said Emily, 'but we'll have to be quick. The buckle is really stiff and if it isn't fastened by the time you change into Spitfire we'll still be in trouble. And what do we do about taking it off again? The trick with the pillow probably won't work a second time.'

The wizard stroked his beard thoughtfully. 'I will ponder on that, but I have no control over Spitfire so I fear that it will continue to be difficult.'

Chapter 27

'Now I must change back into Spitfire,' said the wizard. 'I hope I don't attack you when you remove my collar tomorrow.'

'So do I,' said Emily as she looked at the red marks on her arms, 'and I'm still not sure we can put it on without getting scratched.'

'I think we can,' said James. He picked up the collar and buckled it. 'The tabby cat is smaller than Spitfire so we can just slip it over his head.'

Emily looked at James in surprise. He'd changed. He was no longer the frightened boy who had refused to trust her. He was beginning to think and his ideas were sensible and helpful. 'That's a good idea, as long as it's not too tight,' she said. For the first time since her capture she felt a glimmer of hope. Together, with the wizard's help they might be able to get the better of Ammonia after all.

The transformation from wizard to Spitfire went without a hitch. Emily tried to sleep but she fidgeted so much that Spitfire snarled and leapt across to James's bed. Emily was relieved but she still lay awake. As she went over the events of the day she remembered the locket and the long silver hair. She sat up, shocked and annoyed that she'd failed to mention it. How could she have forgotten something so important? She was certain that it was a clue to Ammonia's new spell, but they'd spent so much time talking about the things that had happened on Witchvision that it had slipped her mind. Dare she try to remove Spitfire's collar again? Or could it wait another day? Just how important was it? She was still pondering on the problem when the whirr of the spiralator cut into her thoughts.

'Wake up,' Ammonia shouted as she pushed into the room. 'It's Exam 500 today and I need an early start. Guess who's going to get a hundred per cent and guess how many witches are going to fail.' She chortled gleefully. 'Come on, move yourselves.'

Emily, who had been awake for most of the night, rubbed her eyes, yawned and sat up. James, startled, but still half-asleep, staggered to his feet and walked unsteadily towards the door. Spitfire followed with the usual low growl rumbling in his throat,

Once they were downstairs Ammonia dashed around in a frenzy of activity.

She packed a bag, shouted for newly sharpened pencils and fresh polish on her boots. She peered into the mirror, combed her hair, examined her warts and twiddled the nine bristles into a single curl.

Right,' she said. 'I'm off. Work on my costume and have a meal ready for the moment I get back. Make it something special. I'll be celebrating.'

'But,' asked Emily, 'how will we know when to expect you? If the meal is ready too soon it'll spoil, and if it isn't ready you'll punish us. Can't you give us an hour's warning?'

Ammonia poked Emily in the ribs. She pushed her backwards with every poke, and when Emily was pressed against the bookshelf, she sneered. 'Think you're clever don't you? Planning something naughty while my back is turned? Hoping to have a warning so I don't catch you up to mischief? Well, it didn't work.'

143

'I wasn't, 'Emily protested. 'I just want the meal to be ready, and anyway, Spitfire won't let us do anything we shouldn't.'

Ammonia poked the cat with the toe of her boot. 'If I find out you've been too lenient,' she said, 'I'll tighten your collar and lock you in the cupboard for a week.'

She turned back to Emily. 'I don't know when I'll be back. It may be tonight or it may be tomorrow. Whenever it is, the meal had better be ready.' With a cackle of laughter and a swirl of her cloak she disappeared.

Emily stared open-mouthed. James ran to the place where Ammonia had passed through the wall. He pushed and pressed, but he gave a gesture of hopelessness when he failed to find a way out.

'Waste of time looking,' said Spitfire. 'You're not going anywhere, and if you know what's good for you, you'll behave yourselves. I'm going to have a proper rest and you'd better not spoil it.'

He lay down on the rug in front of the fire and within seconds he was asleep. Emily settled down to sew the dress while James took up the scissors and started to cut more squares.

'Do you think,' James whispered, 'that we could take Spitfire's collar off?'

'Exactly what I was thinking,' Emily whispered back, 'but he won't fall for the pillow trick again and I can't think of anything else. Besides, this room is so big that we won't be able to catch him if he decides to run.'

'Steak,' said James. 'It's his favourite food. He once got into trouble for stealing some. Ammonia only gives him biscuits now so we might be able to tempt him. Watch this.'

He took a length of strong ribbon from the wicker basket and tied it in a slipknot. Next, he tied a piece of string to a lump of steak from the fridge.

'Now,' he said to Emily, 'dangle the steak over his head and I'll stand behind him. When he looks up I'll slip the noose over his head and tighten it. As soon as I've done that you must drop the steak and unbuckle the collar.'

To Emily's astonishment she found herself smiling. Ammonia was out of the way for at least a day, and James had come up with another brilliant idea. If it worked they could forget about Spitfire for the next few hours. And best of all, they would have the wizard to help them.

'Ready?'

Emily nodded. James stood behind Spitfire with the noose wide open. Emily dangled the steak above the cat's nose. Nothing happened at first, but soon Spitfire's nose began to twitch. He licked his lips, lifted his nose and sniffed. James dropped the noose over his head and at the same moment Emily let go of the steak.

Spitfire pounced on it. He tore it apart, gnawing and chewing as if he hadn't eaten for months. James hung on to the tightened ribbon while Emily unbuckled the collar. From Spitfire to tabby cat, from tabby cat to wizard took but a moment.

'This is wonderful,' said the wizard as he looked round. 'Access to this room is exactly what I need. Now we should find a clue to Ammonia's spell.'

'I already have one,' said Emily. 'What does retribution mean?'

'It means punishing someone for something they've done to you, but why do you ask?'

'Because that's what her spell is about. She's planning to punish someone. It's the word she says when she looks inside her locket.'

'So there's something in the locket that belongs to the person she wants to punish. Do you know what it is?'

'I can't be certain but I think it's a hair. She winds it round her finger and mutters about revenge and retribution. If it is a hair, it's a very long one, and just for a moment, it shone like silver. Besides that, she said her spell would get the better of something beginning with B. Then she stopped as if she'd almost given a secret away.'

The wizard gasped and covered his face with his hands. He was silent for many minutes. When he lowered his hands his face was grave.

'I have alerted my colleagues,' he said, 'and if our suspicions are correct, the situation is far more serious than we anticipated. You have done well, Emily, but we must advance with extreme caution. We must be ready at all times to replace my collar. If Ammonia finds me in this form, there will be an almighty battle and I am by no means certain that I can win.'

Chapter 28

'I must search the room,' said the wizard, 'but first, is there anything I can do to help?'

'If you could magic up some food that would save time and worry,' said Emily. 'Ammonia wants something special for the minute she gets back, but we don't know when to expect her.'

The wizard walked over to the stove, took a wand from his sleeve and tapped a large saucepan. 'There,' he said, 'that's a chicken casserole. 'You can heat it up when she arrives.'

'Could you manage a chocolate cake too?' James asked.

The wizard put a plate on the table and tapped it. The cake appeared by magic. Emily licked her lips at the sight of it. Three layers of buttercream and a thick chocolate topping looked mouth-wateringly splendid.

'Even Ammonia should be satisfied with that,' she said.

'Indeed,' said the wizard, 'but that is the end of the fun. Now we must deal with serious issues. How does Ammonia travel? How does she get in and out of here?'

'She brought me in a flying car,' said Emily. 'She counted to seven and we jumped through the castle doorway and found ourselves in here.'

'It was the same for me,' said James. 'One minute we were outside the old castle and the next we were in this room.'

The wizard sighed. 'The absence of a door makes it almost impossible for us to escape. Her spell for passing through walls will be a complicated one. I must try to decipher it before she returns. Fortunately, my hearing is acute. I will hear the car, so I will have time to change back into Spitfire before she comes through the wall. James, you must be ready to replace the collar at a second's notice. Keep it next to you at all times.'

James picked up the collar, fastened the buckle and looped it over the back of his chair. He picked up the scissors and started to cut more squares. Emily began to sew.

'Now I must see what I can discover,' said the wizard.

Every now and then, Emily looked up to see what he was doing. He went round the room, touching every surface with the tip of his wand. He looked into cupboards, searched along shelves, shook jars and poked his fingers into bags. He opened bottles and sniffed the contents. He spent a long time staring into the small amount of green liquid in the spray bottle. He swirled it around and sniffed, he even put a tiny drop on his finger and tasted it, but Emily could tell by the way he shook his head that he didn't know exactly what was in it.

As he continued his search, James and Emily worked in silence, but gradually they relaxed, and by mid-morning they were starting to talk.

'The worst thing is that my parents must think I'm dead,' said James. 'I bet they stopped looking for me ages ago.'

Emily looked up. 'But they haven't been looking for you. Didn't Ammonia tell you? When she captures you, she stops your time. No-one knows you're missing. Look.' She held out her arm to show her watch. '11.27, that's the time she captured me. When I go home it'll still be 11.27.'

'That's impossible,' said James. 'No-one can stop time, and I don't think you're going home anyway.'

'Ah!' said the wizard as he came across the room. 'Now I understand what these entries mean.'

He handed a notebook to Emily. 'Look, at the last line. EEC. 11.27, 01.06. Are those your initials and is that the date she captured you?'

Emily nodded. 'Yes, I'm Emily Elizabeth Carmichael and it was the 1st of June.'

James snatched the book from her. His muddled thoughts tumbled out one after another. 'Where's my name and when did she capture me? I've been here so long I can't remember. I wasn't wearing a watch so I don't even know what time it was.'

He scanned the list, his finger shaking as it ran down the rows of initials. He'd turned three pages before he read out his entry.

'JHW. 14.50, 17.12. That's me. James Henry Watson. I remember now. I was Christmas shopping and a woman dropped her bag. Her parcels fell out and I picked them up and carried them to her car. The next thing I knew I was strapped inside and we were flying. What a dirty rotten trick.'

He jumped to his feet, threw the scissors down and shouted. 'I hate her.' His breath came in rapid jerks. His face turned red and he began to cry. It was hard to be brave when someone else was so upset. Emily sniffed and tried to hold back her tears, but it was impossible. They flowed down her cheeks, hot and angry.

The wizard put his arms round them both. 'Do not despair,' he said. 'You must be brave for a while longer. Do not do anything to annoy Ammonia. Do not say anything to anger her. Be vigilant and I truly believe that we will discover her secret. Come now, wipe away your tears and tell me what you would like for lunch. '

'Pizza.' They said the same word at exactly the same time. The wizard laughed and despite their tear-stained faces they both managed a watery smile.

'Mushroom, please,' said Emily as she wiped her eyes, 'and vanilla ice cream with toffee sauce.'

James blew his nose. 'Ham and pineapple and the same ice cream, please,' he said.

'I have never tasted pizza or toffee sauce and I am tired of cat biscuits, 'said the wizard. 'So I shall have the same.'

With a flourish of his wand lunch arrived and when the pizza was finished three ice cream sundaes appeared. Soon, they too had been eaten. The wizard cleared the table with another wave of his wand. Then he opened the diary that he'd found before lunch.

'There's an entry for Hallowe'en,' he said. 'It's in a strange language, but I think it's the date for the Festival.'

Emily did a quick calculation and then she groaned. 'But that's four months away! I can't stay here that long. I have to go home.'

'At least there's no rush to get the costume finished,' said James. 'If it's ready too soon she might get rid of us. I think we should slow down.'

'A sensible strategy,' said the wizard, 'but don't make it too slow or she will lose patience.'

'Hallowe'en,' Emily mumbled as she re-threaded her needle. Even if she finished the dress in good time, there was the cloak to embroider. If she made the embroidery really fancy, she could keep going for months. The pictures she'd seen of witches at the last Festival had all been wearing elaborate headdresses, so she would have to make one of those too. The trouble was that she didn't want to do any of it. She didn't want to sew another stitch for the rest of her life. Still, she reminded herself, it was better than being a Devil's coach horse in a disgusting smelly cage.

'Don't cut any more squares,' she said to James. 'Look in the book and see if you can find Joanna Blackstock. Ammonia said she'd gone home, I wonder if she records it in some way.'

'Here she is,' said James after a brief search.' JB, and there's an H after the date. That must mean she's gone home.' He waved the book in front of Emily. 'There are dozens without an H. That means they're still here. We've got to rescue them. We've got to persuade Ammonia to make some more green stuff.'

Emily knotted her cotton and held up the dress. The first sleeve now had seven rows of squares, and although she'd added a few large squares to the bottom of the skirt, there was an enormous amount still to do.

'That's two days work and I've hardly started. I'll tell her I can't finish it on my own. She'll have to give me a helper.' She yawned and flexed her aching fingers. 'It's hard work and I've had enough.' She put down the dress and the needle. 'I'm going to rest while I have the chance.'

151

Chapter 29

The wizard put the notebooks away. He sat close to the fire, gazed into the flames and shook his head. 'I too must rest. I am weary and have made little progress. Everything of importance has been wrapped in layers of secrecy. In the time available I cannot break through them.'

'But if you can't,' asked James, 'is there anyone who can?'

'It seems unlikely,' said the wizard. 'The other Malevolent Witches would love to steal Ammonia's spells, but it would take the combined power of many of them. That will never happen because they are so jealous of their individual power that they never co-operate with one another.'

'What about wizards?'

Emily had only just asked the question when the wizard cried out, 'She's back.'

He leapt from his chair and threw himself on the floor behind the sofa. James grabbed the collar and followed. Emily ran to the stove to light the gas. She stirred the contents of the pan, but all her thoughts were with James and the wizard. She couldn't see what was happening behind the sofa. She stood on tiptoe, but she still couldn't see. Would James get the collar on the tabby cat? Would the tabby cat turn into Spitfire before Ammonia arrived?

To her great relief, James crawled round the corner of the sofa and had just picked up his scissors when Ammonia burst through the wall. Emily daren't look at her. She couldn't still her thumping heart. She couldn't slow her panting breath. She kept her head down and hoped that Ammonia would leave her alone until she'd calmed herself.

'Spitfire, you ugly brute, where are you? Get over here this minute,' Ammonia shouted.

A few seconds passed before Spitfire emerged from behind the sofa. He was shaking his head as if he wasn't sure what had happened. Would Ammonia notice a change in him? Would he say something to make her suspicious?

'Well?' Ammonia demanded. 'Did they behave themselves?'

'Perfectly,' he yawned. 'I haven't taken my eyes off them for a single second. Now I'm tired.' He sauntered to the rug, stretched himself out in front of the fire and instantly fell asleep.

'I'm glad to hear it, but...' She looked round through narrowed eyes, lifted up her nose and sniffed. 'Something's been going on.'

'Just sewing and cooking,' said James. 'We haven't had time for anything else.'

Ammonia whacked the back of the sofa with her stick. 'I don't believe you. You've been snooping.'

Emily crossed her fingers behind her back. 'Of course we haven't. We wouldn't dare. Even if we wanted to, Spitfire wouldn't let us.'

'Well,' Ammonia insisted. 'Something feels different. Something smells different.'

'It's supper,' said Emily. 'We've made your celebration meal.'

'Celebration! What celebration?'

'You said we'd celebrate when you got back,' said Emily. 'You know, one hundred per cent and...'

'Shh,' James whispered. 'Don't say any more. She must have failed.'

'What?' Ammonia grabbed him by the ear. 'How dare you say I failed? I just haven't got the results. The Grand High Witch said there'd been too much cheating and they have to analyse all the papers. They'll announce the results on Witchvision at nine o'clock.'

She let go of James's ear and frowned at Emily. 'I had to hurry back. I didn't have time for your shopping.'

'But you got the fabric glue. Please say you got that.'

'No I didn't. So you'll have to keep sewing, and, Miss Clever Clogs, you'll be pleased to know that you got your own way. There's no wool and no needles. So you won't have to embroider after all.'

She snatched the spoon from Emily and poked the contents of the pan. 'Stew, horrible, boring stew. Why did you make stew when I'd set my heart on a fry-up?'

'Because we didn't know,' said Emily. 'You didn't say what you wanted, and it isn't stew. It's a special chicken casserole. Please try it. I'm sure you'll like it.'

Ammonia did like it, although she didn't say so. They could tell by the way she gobbled two helpings, scraped the pan clean and finally licked her plate. She'd eaten hurriedly, glancing at the clock between mouthfuls as she waited for the exam results. By the time she'd finished eating it was ten minutes to nine. She pushed her plate away, stuck her finger in the chocolate cake and sucked it.

'Not bad,' she said, 'although I really wanted apple crumble.'

She cut herself a huge slice of cake, topped it with two scoops of ice cream and smothered it in cream. She stared at the clock, absentmindedly mashing up the cake and stirring it into a creamy mess. As the clock hands approached nine she pushed back her chair and switched on the television.

Emily and James watched and waited. There was no order to go to bed. Ammonia had forgotten everything except the announcement that was to come. She stared at the screen, leaning forwards and breathing heavily. Suddenly the television beeped. The trumpet fanfare sounded. The word WITCHVISION appeared and was quickly replaced by a group of witches. Eleven of them sat in a semi-circle. In front of them, in an elaborately carved chair sat the twelfth.

Emily grasped James's hand. 'It's The Grand High Council and that must be The Grand High Witch herself,' she whispered.

James averted his eyes. 'She's too hideous for words. I can't look.' He turned his back and covered his ears. Emily picked up her sketchbook and began to design a cloak, but as she drew, she listened, and every now and then she risked a quick glance at the screen.

The trumpets stopped, The Grand High Witch began to speak. 'In all my years as Grand High Witch I have never been so disappointed. Exam 500 was a disaster. Out of two hundred and thirteen entrants, one hundred and forty eight have failed and sixty-two have cheated. It gives me no pleasure to pronounce the death sentence on all of them. It will reduce our numbers considerably but there can be no reprieve. Rules are rules and must be upheld. Both groups will surrender their spells and their Public Elimination will take place here at midnight.'

Emily almost cheered. Eliminating so many witches was good news, but would Ammonia be among them?

The Grand High Witch continued. 'Only three witches have scored one hundred per cent. Congratulations to…' Here she paused.

'Get on with it,' Ammonia muttered between clenched teeth.

There was a drum roll during which Ammonia clutched her chest and cried out. 'It must be me.'

The drum roll faded. The Grand High Witch called out. 'Congratulations to Vitriola P Sniff.'

Ammonia groaned.

'Congratulations to Mandragora M Twitch.'

Ammonia clutched her hair and howled.

'Congratulations to Ammonia B Clickfinger.'

'I knew it,' Ammonia shrieked. 'It had to be me.'

'There is little cause for celebration,' said The Grand High Witch. 'It is a sad state of affairs when only three witches will be allowed to live beyond their four hundred and ninety ninth year.'

A slight murmur of agreement was followed by a great deal of moaning and groaning.

The Grand High Witch raised her hand for silence. 'Old incompetent witches, witches who cheat, witches who are incapable of passing Exam 500 are a burden to our society. They must be eliminated to make way for younger, more dedicated witches. Only then can we maintain the standards that are necessary to our cause.'

She rose from her chair, hobbled to the front of the platform and spoke out loud and clear. 'Now we turn to more serious matters. I believe that The Benevolent Wizards are getting dangerously close to our secrets. At our next Festival, Sniff, Twitch and Clickfinger will compete for the thirteenth chair. When that chair is filled, our strength will double. We need that strength in order to defeat The Benevolent Wizards. This is a matter of extreme urgency. We cannot wait until Hallowe'en. We will therefore hold the Festival at McCaig's Tower, Oban at midnight on the seventh day of the seventh month.'

'No!' Ammonia wailed. 'You can't do that. I'm not ready. All those years of planning and it'll come to nothing. I can't bear it.'

To Emily's surprise, Ammonia covered her face and wept.

Chapter 30

After the initial shock, Ammonia's despair turned to rage. Her angry screams filled the room. The high-pitched sound bounced off the walls making bottles rattle. Spitfire burrowed his head under a cushion. James and Emily covered their ears. The screams went on until Ammonia ran out of breath.

Even then, it was a momentary pause. She stamped round the room, kicking everything that stood in her way. She aimed her foot at Spitfire, but he was too quick for her. He caught the toe of her boot and began to worry it as if it was a dead rat. A moment later, he fell back, gasping for breath.

'He's choking,' said James. 'Quick, do…'

The witch whipped round. 'Who said that?'

'I…I did,' stammered James.

Ammonia yanked him to his feet. 'Why should you care if he chokes and why aren't you in bed?'

Emily cut in before he had time to answer. 'You didn't send us and we can't go by ourselves.'

Ammonia grabbed her by the shoulder. 'So, you heard.'

Emily tried to pull away. 'Heard what?'

'Everything.'

James shrugged. 'I heard a trumpet but when I saw the witch I was so scared that I turned away and covered my ears.'

'But you heard.' Ammonia shook Emily. 'Tell me what you heard.'

'Nothing.' Emily considered for a moment. It was a lie. Ammonia would be more likely to believe her if she admitted something. She looked into Ammonia's eyes. 'Well, hardly anything. I saw the witches and I knew you wouldn't want me to watch, so I didn't. I started designing your cloak and when I'm drawing I forget everything else. I haven't a clue what she said. Did she say you'd passed?'

'Of course I passed. That was never in doubt.'

'So you can do your spell at the Festival.' Emily put on her most excited voice.

'That's brilliant, but why aren't we celebrating?'

'Because it's a disaster. How can I celebrate when they've changed the date? I had four months and now I only have five weeks.'

Emily, pretending that she hadn't heard put her hand to her mouth and gasped. 'No. That's not fair, but surely you're going to try.'

'What's the point? I'll never be ready. I might as well give up.'

'That's a shame,' said James. 'If you finish it, I'm sure you'll win.'

'But there's too much to do and not enough time,' she wailed, 'and even if I master my spell, will my costume be ready?'

Emily shook her head. 'Not a chance, not without fabric glue, and not if there's only James to help me. But we can't give up now. We've got to think of something.'

There was a long pause. Ammonia scratched her head. James walked round the room as if he was deep in thought. Emily doodled in her sketchbook. She knew the answer. It was obvious and it was perfect. They needed more help and that would mean making more Reverse Transformation Potion.

'I can't see a way round it,' said Ammonia as she picked her nose with her long black fingernail. 'Can't you think of anything?'

'I've got one idea,' said Emily, 'but I don't think you'll like it. Supposing you had a couple of people to help with your spell, supposing I had a few people to help with your costume, and supposing we had a couple of people to cook and clean, you might stand a chance.'

'That's an awful lot of supposing and an awful lot of helpers,' Ammonia grumbled. 'It's a possibility but I haven't the energy.'

'If I were you, I'd give it my best shot,' said James, 'especially when you consider the alternative.'

'No,' said Emily. 'Forget it. Leave her alone. If she doesn't feel up to it we can't force her.'

'Well, I'm surprised,' said James. 'I didn't think she'd give up without even trying.'

Ammonia thumped the table and shouted. 'Stop talking about me as if I'm not here. But you're right. I won't give in. I'll show them what Ammonia B Clickfinger can do, but you'll have to help. Let's give it our…what did you call it?'

'Best shot,' they said in unison.

'We'll get more helpers tomorrow,' said Ammonia. 'I'm too tired to do anything tonight.'

'No,' said Emily. 'We can't waste time. Get the helpers now then they can start work in the morning.'

Ammonia yawned. Her mouth opened so wide that Emily could see the stumps of rotting teeth. The smell of her foul breath drifted across the room and Emily turned her head to avoid breathing the awful stench.

Ammonia yawned again. 'I suppose you're right. Get some green sprays while I decide who'll be most useful.'

She went to the bookshelf, took out the logbook and ran her finger down the list of captive children. 'Here,' she passed a pencil and paper to James, 'write down the names when I call them out.'

Emily brought the green spray bottle that had been used on Joanna and James.

'I'm afraid this is the last one,' she said as she handed it to Ammonia. 'It's almost empty, but never mind. You can make some more.'

'Not tonight,' Ammonia moaned.

'Yes, tonight,' Emily insisted. 'Do you want to perform your spell, or not?'

'Of course I do.'

'Then let us help,' said James.

Ammonia considered for a moment. 'All right. You've convinced me. James, get the biggest cauldron, the largest spoon and a measuring jug. Emily, get the weigh scales.'

They hurried to do her bidding and by the time everything was ready, Ammonia was poring over a small leather-bound book. Where it had been hidden they had no idea. The wizard certainly hadn't managed to find it.

'This is a ridiculously huge quantity,' Ammonia grumbled, 'but I can't reduce it because it needs a whole sheep's head complete with eyes. It's going to take hours to bottle it all.'

'Never mind,' Emily yawned. 'We're tired but we'll stay up all night if we have to.'

'Right,' said Ammonia. 'Put seven litres of water in the cauldron and light the gas. Then add seven bottles of blue potion and seven bottles of yellow. James, you keep stirring and tell me when it comes to the boil.'

Surprisingly, Ammonia seemed to have overcome her tiredness. She buzzed round the room, rummaging in cupboards for paper packets, scooping small amounts out of each one. She collected jars from shelves and weighed out larger quantities. She tipped them all into a bowl and told Emily to mix them well.

As she stirred Emily tried to work out what the things were. Some were herbs, others looked like tiny dried beetles, and some were definitely little pink grubs.

'It's starting to simmer,' James called.

'Keep stirring,' said Ammonia as she tipped the contents of Emily's bowl into the cauldron.

As soon as the mixture began to boil, the witch clicked her finger. What happened next was so sudden that Emily barely caught a glimpse of the sheep's head. It flew through the air, eyes staring as if it was still alive. It dropped into the cauldron with a splash, and as it sank, a stinking vapour rose into the air

'Quick James, keep stirring,' Ammonia yelled. 'This is the crucial part.'

James stirred and stirred. Emily watched as the liquid fizzed, bubbled and rose up until it almost poured over the sides of the cauldron. It heaved and plopped like boiling porridge, but it wasn't green at all. It was a very murky brown.

Chapter 31

Emily and James stared in dismay. The potion was the wrong colour, but Ammonia didn't seem concerned.

'Stop stirring,' she said. 'Leave it for ten minutes while we have some chocolate cake. I was too worried to eat before. Now we've got a plan I'll be able to enjoy it.'

Ten minutes passed while they tucked into the wizard's wonderful chocolate cake. Soon they were scraping the last few morsels off their plates and licking the remaining crumbs from their lips. Ammonia led the way back to the cauldron. She put a plastic container beside the hob, placed a sieve on top and handed a ladle to James. Next to these she placed a funnel and a carton of empty spray bottles. Finally, she gave the potion a stir.

'Perfect,' she said. 'It's turned green. Filter it through the sieve and then bottle it, but be careful. I don't want any spills.'

Off she went, into the corner, banging the floor with her stick and pulling a bunch of keys from her pocket. 'Oops!' she said as she turned back. 'I forgot. Spitfire.' She pushed the protesting cat into the cupboard and locked the door. 'I know you'd like to eat the tasty little beasties, but we have other plans for them this time.'

Emily gasped. Surely Ammonia didn't let Spitfire… She couldn't possibly allow the cat to… The very idea made her tummy heave. The chocolate cake had been a bad idea. She retched, dashed to the sink and was violently sick.

'Clear up that mess and get on with the bottling,' Ammonia shouted. 'You're too sensitive by half.' Chuckling to herself she disappeared among the cages,

James handed Emily a tissue and a glass of water. 'Don't let her upset you,' he whispered.

Emily rinsed her mouth and wiped her face. 'Thanks, James. I'm glad you're here. If I was on my own I don't know what I'd do.'

'Well I am here, so cheer up and soon there'll be more of us.'

A dozen bottles had been filled when Ammonia arrived with an armful of boxes. 'Leave the rest,' she said. 'You can finish bottling tomorrow. Look what I've got. Two to help me, two to cook and clean, and two to sew.'

'That's not enough,' said Emily. 'I need two for the cloak and two for the dress. And if you have James as one of your helpers I'll need someone to replace him.'

Ammonia looked puzzled. 'Why do I need James and why do you need to replace him?'

'Because he's a good worker, he's used to you now and he won't make mistakes,' said Emily. 'And I need to replace him because he does the cutting out and my sewing helpers won't have time.'

'Now I'm confused,' said Ammonia. 'How many is that altogether?'

'Eight,' said Emily.

Ammonia squinted through narrowed eyes. 'Six.'

'If you want the work done in time we need eight. You concentrate on your spell and I'll make sure the helpers behave themselves.'

'What? A pip-squeak like you! Don't be ridiculous. They won't be scared, and if they're not scared they won't do as they're told.'

Emily put her hands on her hips. 'You don't get it, do you? You don't get the best out of people by scaring them. You have to be kind and fair.'

Ammonia snorted. 'Kind? Fair? You don't know what you're talking about.'

'She does,' said James. 'Think about it. What happened to all the children you captured?'

'They made mistakes and got what they deserved,' said Ammonia. 'They should have been more careful.'

'But don't you see? They couldn't be careful because they were scared,' said James. 'That's what happened to me. I was so frightened that my hands were shaking. That's why I made a mistake.'

The witch stamped her foot. 'You're both getting too big for your boots. You're trying to boss me about. I'm in charge and don't you forget it.'

'We couldn't forget it, 'said Emily. 'We just want to help. Leave the children to me. Please.'

Ammonia drummed her fingers on the table. She twiddled her thumbs and clicked her tongue as if she wasn't sure what to do.'

'We're wasting time,' said James. 'We should have started Reverse Transformation by now. Why don't you give Emily a trial? See what she can do in forty-eight hours, and if she can't manage, you can take over.'

'Twenty-four hours,' said Ammonia.

'No,' said Emily, 'twenty-four isn't enough to prove anything.'

Ammonia leapt to her feet. 'See this,' she screeched as she waved her clickfinger in front of their noses. 'It's itching to click and it's not thinking of transformation. It's set on eliminating the pair of you, and if I didn't need you, I'd let it.'

She sat down heavily. 'All right, forty-eight hours, but not a second longer. Now let's get the job done. Bring the beasties.'

James opened the first box. There was a frantic scurrying and a great deal of squeaking. Emily bent down. 'Hush,' she said. 'I won't hurt you. Lie still while I lift you out.' Very gently she cupped the frightened mouse in her hands. Its tiny heart thudded against her palms. Her own heart thudded too, not with fear but with anxiety. What would they do if the Reverse Transformation failed?

As soon as the mouse lay still Ammonia covered it in green spray. James, who had not seen reverse transformation before, came a step closer. His eyes widened as the liquid turned to foam and the foam bubbled and grew. When it finally exploded Ammonia shouted, 'Cut.'

In place of the mouse lay a small, bewildered girl. Emily bent over and lifted her up.

'Put her down,' yelled Ammonia.

Emily ignored the order. She sat the girl on the sofa and put her arm round her.

Ammonia yelled even louder. 'Don't you dare disobey me?'

'I'm not,' said Emily. 'You agreed to give me forty-eight hours and I've only had two minutes. I'm being kind and fair. She's had a shock and if I treat her properly she'll be a good helper. I promise.'

'Try not to worry,' she said to the girl. 'I'm going to help you.' She glared at Ammonia and added, 'and that's a promise too.'

'Bat's blood and warlock's whiskers,' Ammonia fumed. 'I never said you could mollycoddle them.'

'You said I could do it my way,' said Emily, 'and this is it.'

James ended the argument by bringing two more creatures. 'Just lie still,' he said as he set them down. 'You'll be back to normal soon.'

Ammonia sniffed and scowled and twitched her nose, but she picked up the spray and aimed it at the big brown cockroach. When it had transformed into a boy, she sprayed the lizard. That turned into a boy too. Next, James brought a hedgehog and a gerbil. Both of these turned into girls. Emily helped them onto the sofa. She spoke softly, reassuring them, telling them not to look at Ammonia.

When James lifted the lid of the last box he clutched his chest and staggered back. 'I can't touch it,' he gasped.

The moment she saw the horror on James's face, Emily guessed what he'd seen. She still shuddered at the thought of touching a slug, but she'd done it once and she'd do it again. As her fingers closed on the slimy body, it drew in its tentacles and shrank into a fat black blob. Carefully she put it down in front of Ammonia.

James clutched her hand and his voice cracked with emotion. 'This is what happened to me,' he said. He watched in horrified fascination as the slug squirmed, the slimy green froth bubbled and grew until, with a flash, a bang and a billow of green smoke, it exploded.

'Cut,' shouted Ammonia.

James gasped. 'Peter. It's you. I'm so glad it's you.' He flung his arms round the boy and hugged him.' He looked up at Emily, his eyes bright with tears. 'It's my brother,' he said. 'It's my brother and I didn't know he was here.'

Chapter 32

Emily looked round at the new children. James sat in the armchair holding onto Peter as if he'd never let go. The other five children huddled on the sofa, clutching one another's hands, their faces pale and drawn. Despite their worried expressions, Emily was thrilled. They'd done it. They'd persuaded Ammonia to release six children. She put her hand over her mouth to hide the smile that was spreading from ear to ear. But when she thought of all the other children waiting to be rescued, the smile disappeared more quickly than it had arrived.

'I know you're scared,' she said, 'but if you work hard and keep quiet, Ammonia will let me be in charge of you. If you don't behave, she'll take over and you know what that means. So please do as I say. Now, James will get milk and biscuits for you while I help Ammonia to get two more children.'

'Not on your life,' Ammonia shouted. 'Not another one. We're over-run as it is, and James, stay where you are. They don't need milk and biscuits. Take them to bed and make sure they're ready for work in the morning.'

'Not without the other two,' said Emily, 'and they need to eat. If you want them to work we'll have to build up their strength.'

The children stared in amazement. Their mouths fell open, their eyes, wide and terrified, darted from Emily to Ammonia and back to Emily again.

'There won't be another two,' snapped the witch, 'get that into your stubborn head. James and his brother can help me. One can cook and clean. That

169

leaves four for you. That's enough to get everything done.'

Emily looked along the row of anxious faces. 'No,' she said, 'four isn't enough. There are extra mouths to feed so we need two to cook and clean. You agreed to that in the first place.'

'All right,' Ammonia groaned, 'if we have two to cook you'll have to manage with three.'

Emily shrugged. 'OK,' she said as if she didn't care one way or the other. 'But you've taken James from me so we'll have to do the cutting and make your hat as well as the dress. We'll try our best but it won't be anything special. There won't be anyone left to work on a cloak. That's a shame because you can't make a really grand entrance without a cloak. Still, as long as you're happy…'

'But I'm not happy,' Ammonia roared. 'I've never been so unhappy in my life. Look at me, taking orders from a little bitty slip of a girl. If my father could see me now he'd die of shock if he wasn't dead already.'

She sat down at the table, rested her head on one hand and mumbled a string of words. Among them Emily heard revenge – hate – punish, and that word again – retribution.

As she mumbled Ammonia fingered something that lay hidden inside her dress. Now Emily had another clue to the spell. The locket! Ammonia had touched it when she mentioned her father. The spell must be something to do with him.

She got up and went across the room, and although she had to pluck up courage to do it, she patted the witch's shoulder. 'Don't worry. We can do it all if you just give me two more helpers. That's all I need to

170

make your costume truly magnificent. Just imagine what it'll be like at the Festival. There'll be a fanfare of trumpets. You'll walk onto the stage in a long black cloak covered in sparkling stars. You'll fling it open to show a silver lining and when they see your dress, every single witch will cheer.'

Ammonia's eyes seemed to brighten, but only for a moment. She yawned and looked at the clock. 'It's almost three o'clock,' she said. 'The night's half gone.' She tried to rise to her feet, but she sat down again and sighed. She pointed to the room where the transformed children lay in their assorted cages. 'I haven't the energy to go in there again. I wouldn't know who to pick and I'm too tired to search through the log-book again.'

'Let me choose,' said Emily. 'I'm sure I can find two people who can sew.'

Ammonia dropped her head on the table. 'I'm too exhausted to think. Go on, but don't take all night.'

Before Ammonia could change her mind, Emily was inside the awful room among the cages. The thought of so many children trapped inside unfamiliar bodies sickened her. She ought to be rescuing every single one of them. How could she possibly choose two?

'Listen,' she said. 'I'm here to help you.'

There was a rustling of straw and a few excited squeaks and grunts.

'I can only take two of you and you're not going home. I need two people who can sew. Don't say you can if you can't or we'll all be in trouble.'

The sounds changed to moans and groans that gradually faded into silence. Emily's eyes filled with tears. Her voice, when she finally spoke, was shaking. 'I wish I could take you all, but I'll come back as soon as I can. So, please be patient, and if you really can sew let me see you.'

Mostly there was silence, but from the far corner came an unmistakable scratching sound. She hurried between the cages, and there, as alike as two peas in a pod, two rabbits scrabbled at the netting of their cage.

Emily knelt down. 'Are you sure you can sew?'

The rabbits sat back on their haunches. Their ears pricked up, their pink noses twitched, their eyes stared into Emily's and their heads nodded. Emily opened the cage, lifted them into her arms and carried them to Ammonia.

'Please do the reverse transformation,' she said, 'then we can all go to bed.'

Ammonia struggled to her feet and sprayed, first one and then the other. Within a couple of minutes the rabbits had turned into identical twin girls.

'That's it. I've had enough. Get to bed,' ordered Ammonia. 'Now.'

She locked the door of the zoo, let Spitfire out of the cupboard and called the spiralator. James dashed to the kitchen and filled a basket with tumblers, milk and biscuits. Emily shepherded the eight children onto the spiralator. Spitfire, coughing because of the tightness of his collar, trailed behind. When they reached the corridor, Emily helped the exhausted children along. She unlocked the door and as it opened, the room expanded. Instead of two beds there were ten.

'I wondered where we were going to sleep,' said James. 'I might have guessed, but it still beats me how she does it.'

Emily locked the door and attached the key to Spitfire's collar, but he gave her a nasty scratch when she tried to unfasten the buckle. So she left him alone while she helped James to hand round the milk and biscuits. As soon as the eight children were settled she turned her attention back to the cat. He was wheezing dreadfully but he still wouldn't let her touch his collar.

Desperately she called to James. 'Come and hold him down. He'll die if we don't get his collar off.'

'Let him die,' said one of the boys, 'he's vicious and cruel. He gave me this awful scratch.' He pulled back his sleeve to show a festering wound. 'I've had it for ages and it won't heal. Why on earth do you want to save him?'

'Don't say that.' James retorted angrily. 'You don't understand.'

The cat gave one last gasp, closed his eyes and lay still. There was no need for James to hold him. With shaking fingers Emily hurriedly unfastened the buckle. Slowly, very slowly, Spitfire changed into a tabby cat.

'See,' said James, 'he's not Spitfire at all. He's under a spell. He's not even a cat. In a minute he'll change into a wizard.'

But the cat lay still and the wizard did not appear.

Chapter 33

'Do something,' Emily cried as she stroked the unconscious cat. 'We've got to save him. He's the only one who can help us to escape.'

The twins jumped off their beds.

'Out of the way,' said one.

'Our mum's a vet,' said the other. 'We know what to do.'

They bent so low over the tabby cat that Emily couldn't see what was happening. She heard sharp puffs of breath. Then, after what seemed a very long time the cat gasped and began to pant. A few minutes later, his breathing returned to normal. He rose unsteadily to his feet and changed into the wizard. Emily burst into tears of relief and rushed into his arms.

'Don't cry,' he said. 'These young ladies have saved my life.' He grasped their hands, thanked them warmly and turned to the other children.

'I am pleased to see you all, but you are not yet free from Ammonia's spells. However, take heart, for we are working towards sending you home.'

For the first time since they'd resumed their own shape, the children's eyes flickered with hope.

'But,' the wizard continued, 'success depends on you and the way you behave. You must not speak a word of my transformation. If Ammonia has the slightest inkling of my true identity there will be no escape for anyone. You must do as Emily bids you. Work hard and go about your tasks quietly and diligently.'

Although the children nodded to show that they understood, their worried expressions returned.

In an effort to cheer them up, Emily forced a smile. 'At least you're better off than you were. Now we must get to know one another and decide which jobs you're going to do. Making meals is probably the most difficult. Is there anyone who likes cooking?'

The children looked round at one another, either unsure of their cooking skills or nervous about being the first to speak.

Eventually, a ginger-haired boy put up his hand. 'I'm Ben. My dad has a restaurant so I've learned quite a lot about cooking.'

'That's great,' said Emily. 'You can be head cook. You'll have someone to work with you, but you'll both have to do the cleaning as well.'

Ben pulled a face. 'I'm not keen on that, but I won't complain.'

Emily, wondering how she would ever tell the twins apart, gave them a smile of encouragement. They nudged one another, each trying to make the other speak.

One of them finally gave in. 'She's Heather and I'm Hazel, but we don't mind if you mix us up. Even our parents do that sometimes,'

'You chose us because we can sew,' said Heather.

'That's right,' said Emily. 'You'll be helping to make a special costume for Ammonia, but we need two more to help us.'

'I'm Justin and I'm quite good at crafts,' said the tallest boy. 'I like making hats, but I don't sew. I use things like wire and pincers.'

'Fantastic,' said Emily. 'You can do the hat. Now we need someone to help Ben in the kitchen.'

A girl about the same age as Emily raised her hand. 'I'm Lisa and I can make soup and easy things like scrambled eggs and fairy cakes. I'm not very good at proper dinners, but I'll try if Ben shows me what to do.'

'That's good enough for me,' said Emily.

She turned to the last two girls. 'I asked for eight children, she said, 'but I didn't think I'd get them. I need one of you to sew. The other's a sort of spare, she can do some cutting out and help wherever an extra pair of hands is needed. Do you mind which?'

The smallest girl took a nervous breath and spoke hesitantly. 'Could that be me? I'm Rosie. I don't know how to sew but I like cutting out and I don't mind washing up.' She looked anxiously at the other girl. 'Is that all right with you?'

The last girl shrugged. 'I'm Megan. I'll do my best to sew, but I hope it's not embroidery.'

'There's lots of plain sewing,' said Emily, 'so don't worry. Straight stitches will be fine.'

'That just leaves us,' said James. 'I think you all know that I'm James and this is my brother Peter. We have to help Ammonia.'

'Now that is settled, you must go to bed,' said the wizard.' The night is almost over, but I will make sure that you are well rested.' He took out his wand, and without including Emily and James, he very gently put the other children to sleep.

He sat on Emily's bed and beckoned James to join them. 'The children will wake when Ammonia comes through the door, but they will sleep well and for a few hours they will be at peace. As for you, I am proud of all you have achieved today, but is there anything else I should know?'

'Yes,' said Emily. 'When Ammonia mentioned her father she fiddled with her locket. I think someone killed him and she wants to get her revenge.'

The wizard put his palms together and bowed his head. Emily and James knew that he was communicating with his fellow wizards. They waited until he lowered his hands and began to speak.

'James, you will be assisting Ammonia, so you have the best chance of discovering the secrets of her spell. Emily, you will be busy, but be vigilant too. I hope that by tomorrow night we will have discovered something to our advantage. Now, replace my collar and let us rest.'

Soon, Spitfire and James were asleep. Emily lay awake for a long time. She thought of all that had happened during the day and of what might happen tomorrow. She would need eyes in the back of her head in order to sew and supervise the helpers. Finding time to keep an eye on Ammonia would be difficult, but that was probably the most important task of all.

'Get up and stand by your beds,' yelled Ammonia as she burst through the door in the early morning.

The eight children were instantly awake. They scrambled to their feet and stood in silence with their heads bowed. Ammonia paced along in front of them, her eyebrows raised as if she was extremely surprised.

'What? No weeping. No wailing. No shivering in your shoes. Well,' she looked at Emily approvingly. 'It seems you've done a good job – so far. Spitfire, lead the way. I'll bring up the rear.'

Spitfire seemed subdued. He didn't spit and snarl. Perhaps, thought Emily, he was feeling sorry for himself after the ordeal of the previous night. Or maybe he was resentful of the way Ammonia had treated him. Whatever it was, she was glad that he wasn't adding to the children's worries. When she stepped off the spiralator she saw that Ammonia had been casting spells again. The room had grown much larger, so too had the table. Eleven chairs stood round it and it was set with eleven bowls of steaming porridge. Ammonia sat down at the head of the table and directed Emily to the other end.

'Sit down and eat,' she ordered. 'You have five minutes and then you must start work.'

Chapter 34

The children ate their porridge to the sound of Ammonia's loud slurping. She rushed through her meal, and before she'd swallowed the last mouthful she shouted at the children.

'Spoons down. Emily take your sewing gang. James and Peter finish bottling. Cooks, come with me.'

With an anxious glance at Emily, Ben and Lisa followed Ammonia to the kitchen.

'Cook whatever you like,' said the witch. 'I'll make the porridge but you must do the rest, a light lunch at one and a main course and pudding at six. You can take drinks and biscuits upstairs for supper. Decide what you want to cook and the ingredients will appear in the fridge, the freezer or the store cupboard. Now get on with it.'

She turned away and shouted for Spitfire. 'Get over here, you lazy brute and make sure that no-one misbehaves.'

The cat, with his head hung low, gave a low growl as he crossed the room. He clambered, rather uncertainly and stretched himself out on the sofa back. He looked down at the sewing gang, but he seemed to have difficulty in keeping his eyes open. Emily, watching him, was filled with concern. Something was wrong, but until they were back in the bedroom, she could do nothing about it. Was it Spitfire or the tabby cat that was unwell? Or even more worrying, was it the wizard?

Ammonia's voice, complaining about lack of space, cut into her thoughts. Peeping through the curtain of her hair, Emily saw shelves sliding apart and an entire wall receding. She saw how, with a click of her finger, Ammonia turned the new space into a science laboratory. She frowned in frustration. The new area was so far away that she couldn't see what Ammonia was doing. She would have to rely on James and Peter to discover the secrets of the spell.

Feeling cheated out of the most important task, she turned back to the sewing gang. At least they'd understood her instructions and were working busily. Rosie, sitting cross-legged by the fire was cutting out stars. Justin was sketching ideas for Ammonia's hat. Heather and Megan were sewing squares onto the dress. Hazel was stitching a large silver star onto the black cloak. Impressed by the neat blanket stitch, Emily nodded her approval.

She too began to work on the cloak, but she glanced up every few minutes. She had to know what everyone was doing. James and Peter were still bottling Reverse Transformation Potion, but by twelve thirty they'd finished. Emily looked on with satisfaction as they placed the precious bottles on a shelf. When the chance came, they would be ready to rescue the other children.

Delicious smells drifted from the kitchen. Justin had sketches waiting for Ammonia's approval. On the stroke of one, Ben banged a pan lid to signal that lunch was ready. They gathered at the table and sat down to bowls of creamy mushroom soup with crispy croutons and hunks of crusty garlic bread.

The children kept their heads down. Such chilling silence made Emily ache for the chatter that accompanied school meals. She clutched her chest as longing for her mum came like a great aching emptiness. But just then, Ammonia ordered them back to work, and a surge of hatred pushed the feeling away. The children hadn't finished eating, some of them had only just been served, but the witch, who had been served first, didn't care.

Emily gripped the edge of the table, 'But…'

The witch stopped her with a look of such anger that Emily had to clamp her lips together. It was the only way she could stop herself from answering back. Even so, she had to ask for a decision about the hat, and she forced herself to hold up the sketches for the witch to see.

'No time,' snapped Ammonia as she snatched the sheets of paper and threw them down. 'I can't be distracted now.'

'But…'

'No buts. Choose the dratted hat yourself. Just make sure it's spectacular.'

Emily persisted. 'We need wire and pliers and…'

'Tool box,' yelled Ammonia, 'under the kitchen sink. Help yourselves and don't bother me again.'

In the quietest of whispers, Emily and Justin agreed on a conical shape. It would be black with stars to match the cloak. There would be rosettes on the wide brim and streamers trailing from the top – all of them matching the colours in the dress.

Everyone worked through the afternoon, and again after the evening meal. It was too much. Emily was tired and she could see that the youngest ones were almost asleep. So it was a great relief when Ammonia called a halt.

Apparently too busy to leave her work she roared across the room. 'Bedtime. Spitfire. Spiralator.'

The supper basket had already been packed, but in a moment of sudden inspiration Emily grabbed cheese and biscuits, a bottle of apple juice, a bag of salad, and a slice of coffee cake. Just in time, she leapt onto the spiralator, and a few minutes later they were back in their room. She attached the key to Spitfire's collar and left the children to choose what they wanted to do.

After working a twelve-hour day, the younger ones, too tired to think about supper, threw themselves on their beds and were soon asleep. Emily went back to Spitfire who was lying on her bed with his eyes closed. Very gently she unbuckled his collar.

'See, he didn't try to stop me,' she said to James. 'He's definitely ill.'

As she spoke he changed into the tabby cat and then into the wizard, but the slowness of the change confirmed that something was wrong.

She laid her hand on his arm. 'What's the matter? Are you ill? Is there anything we can do to help?'

The wizard rubbed his throat and massaged the back of his neck. 'She tightened the collar again. I barely moved all day because I could hardly breath. Besides that, it was too tight for me to swallow. I have had nothing to eat or drink since yesterday. But that is over now.' He reached hungrily for a biscuit.

Emily put her hand out to stop him. 'I have something better,' she said. 'Here, I'm sure this will help.'

He took a long drink. 'Indeed it does. Now, while I eat you can tell me what you have discovered today.'

'Nothing,' said Emily. 'Ammonia made the room bigger and she was so far away that I couldn't see what she was doing.'

'That is a bitter disappointment,' said the wizard as he turned to James. 'But weren't you helping her? Surely you gathered some information about her spell.'

James shook his head sadly. 'I'm sorry. I tried to read her notes but I couldn't get close enough. She made me weigh and measure things but she handed me the bottles so quickly that I didn't have time to read the labels.'

Peter, reluctant to leave James's side was leaning sleepily against his brother. 'Deadly nightshade,' he said with a yawn. 'Mandrake, hemlock, henbane, thorn apple, yew berries and giant hogweed.'

'Excellent, said the wizard, 'but how did you remember?'

'I kept saying the names in my head. I had to grind things up with a pestle and mortar. Then I had to put them back in the same packets. I thought I could mix them up and spoil her spell but she only gave me one at a time so I couldn't.'

'I am relieved to hear it,' said the wizard.

'She'd have eliminated you,' James gasped, 'and then what would I have done? You mustn't do anything to make her angry. Do exactly as she tells you and don't even think of wrecking her spell. The wizards need her to complete it.'

Peter looked as if he was about to cry. 'I'm sorry,' he sniffed. 'I thought we were trying to stop her.'

'We are indeed,' said the wizard, 'but it is too dangerous an undertaking for you. You remembered the names of the ingredients and that is valuable information. Now, replace my collar and go to sleep. We can do no more this night.'

Chapter 35

As days passed Emily struggled to keep her temper. Ammonia was working them so hard that the strain was beginning to show. They never had time to finish their meals and they weren't getting enough rest. The sewing gang had sore fingers and strained eyes. James and Peter had aching wrists from all the grinding, and some of the poisons had given them blisters.

Ammonia, engrossed with calculations and increasingly smelly potions, rarely left the laboratory. Most of the children were free from her prying eyes and scathing comments. Only James and Peter had the ordeal of spending every day under her critical eyes. But even though they watched Ammonia's every move, the nature and purpose of the spell remained a secret.

Despite their weariness, Emily's sewing gang made steady progress with the costume, but the work was tedious and there was still a lot to do. Justin who had taken measurements from one of Ammonia's hats, made a basic shape after many false starts. He covered the cone shape with black fabric and was ready to start on the rosettes and streamers. Rosie, when she wasn't cutting out stars, was a willing kitchen maid. No one made mistakes and to Emily's surprise no one got upset. It was as if they were working in a trance. Emily's main concern was Spitfire. Every night she gave him a meal and loosened his collar, but he spent entire days looking listless and miserable. Thankfully, Ammonia was too involved with her spell to notice the change in him.

Each night, the wizard asked if they had any news, but as day merged into day there was nothing to report.

James always gave the same answer. 'Nothing, absolutely nothing.'

At this, the wizard shook his head despairingly and held long silent conversations with his fellow wizards.

On the fourth day of the fourth week, Ammonia leapt to her feet and shouted triumphantly. 'I've got it.'

Emily looked across at James. He was standing behind Ammonia, shrugging his shoulders as if he had no idea what she was talking about. But Ammonia seemed sure of herself. She danced round the table and demanded a double ice cream sundae. The children glanced enviously at the smothering of toffee sauce and the topping of chocolate buttons and coloured sprinkles.

Emily, with her mouth watering, left her sewing and approached the table. 'The children have worked really hard. I think they deserve some ice cream too.'

'You think! Who gave you permission the think?' Ammonia roared. 'I'm the one who has produced the most amazing spell. I'm the only one who deserves a treat.'

Emily backed away. She'd mis-read the signs. She'd done what she'd told the other children not to do. She'd thoughtlessly angered Ammonia and there was no telling what would happen next. She returned to her sewing, hoping beyond hope that Ammonia would calm down.

But Ammonia didn't calm down. She threw her spoon across the room and pushed her bowl so hard that it clattered to the floor and smashed. 'Now see what you made me do,' she screamed. 'Get over here and clean up the mess.'

Emily looked round at the frightened faces. A shudder ran down her back as she went to pick up the pottery shards. Ammonia stood over her, breathing heavily, her hands on her hips. Then she stuck out her foot and tripped Emily up.

'Getting too big for your boots again, Emily Elizabeth Carmichael,' she sneered.

'That was mean,' called a small clear voice.

'Who said that?' Ammonia whipped round and glared. 'Whoever said that had better own up or I'll punish the lot of you.'

Rosie put down her scissors and stood up. Emily struggled to her feet. Justin slammed the hat down and stood next to Emily. The rest of the sewing gang followed. James and Peter left the laboratory. Ben and Lisa came out of the kitchen and they all surrounded Rosie.

Ammonia's mouth fell open. Her clickfinger rose into the air. It trembled and shook and pointed from one child to the other. She clutched it, struggling to keep it still, and then she forced her way through the children to find Rosie.

James blocked her way. 'Leave her alone, or we'll strike,' he said.

'You'll what?' Ammonia screamed.

'Strike,' said James. 'It means we won't work.'

For the second time, Ammonia was speechless. She stared as James sat down, crossed his arms and lowered his head. The others did exactly the same. Only Emily stared into the witch's eyes. Inside her head she repeated her chosen words. 'Leave Rosie alone or we'll stop working and you'll never be ready for the Festival.'

Ammonia stared back, her eyes piercing Emily's brain, foraging around for some sign of weakness, but Emily refused to be intimidated. Ammonia eventually dropped her eyes and looked at the bowed heads of the other children. She sighed and shook her head.

'To think it should come to this,' she groaned. 'Get back to work, all of you.'

'No,' said Emily. 'Not until you promise not to punish Rosie.'

The witch's long howl of protest ended in a whimper. 'You've won this time. There'll be no punishment but there'll be no ice cream either. You say you've been working hard, now prove it. I want to see my costume.'

Emily's heart sank. The finished parts of the dress looked splendid but there were still large areas of pink waiting to be covered. Shaking with nerves she held up the cloak.

Ammonia twisted her nose this way and that. 'Hm!' she said. 'Is that all? '

'No, of course not,' said Emily. 'There'll be lots more stars.'

Ammonia sniffed. 'Not bad,' she conceded, 'but I want more sparkle.'

'Sequins,' Emily suggested, 'hundreds of sequins between the stars.'

'Not hundreds, thousands,' Ammonia insisted. 'Now, where's the hat?'

Justin held up the black shape. The tall cone with its wide brim was now strong enough to bear the weight of streamers. But it was plain black with only a few stars attached.

'Boring,' she snapped. 'I want things.' She lifted her hands and made twiddly shapes in the air. 'Things that curl round my head. Snakes. That's what I want. Snakes that look as if they're writhing about, snakes that match the colours in the dress.'

She dismissed Justin with a wave of her arm and turned to Emily. 'Now for the dress.'

With her heart thumping, Emily held it up. Ammonia's face turned from red to purple.

'How dare you? I said no pink!'

Emily struggled to keep calm. 'You said you wanted every single colour…'

'Except pink,' Ammonia roared.

'Exactly,' said Emily, 'but I had to have a dress to stitch all the other colours onto. Pink was the only one left.'

'I won't have it.' Ammonia snatched it from Emily's grasp and was about to fling it in the fire when Emily snatched it back and ran behind the sofa.

Ammonia screamed and tore her hair. The sewing gang flinched and trembled. The twins clung to one another. Megan put her arm round Rosie. Emily waited for Ammonia's tantrum to subside, and when the ranting finally stopped she held up the dress. Too exhausted to argue, Ammonia stared at it.

'Please, look at the finished part, 'said Emily. 'You can't see any pink. The witches won't be able to see any pink. No-one will know there's a pink dress underneath.'

'I'll know,' Ammonia wailed, 'and it's all my stupid mother's fault. When I was a kid everything was pink.

Walls, carpets, curtains, sheets, clothes, shoes, even my knickers were pink. She thought pink could stop me from being a witch. When she died I swore I'd never wear pink again, and I won't. You'll have to start again.'

Chapter 36

That night the wizard looked ill and weary. He didn't ask his usual question, but James couldn't wait to tell him the news.

'She's done it,' he said. 'It's amazing. It was a filthy stinking mess and we boiled it...'

'And it turned into vapour,' said Peter. 'It changed into a million colours, then it condensed and ran down the pipe and when the drips dropped out they were silver.'

'She said it was the most amazing spell of all time,' said Emily, 'but we still don't know how she's going to use it.'

The wizard stroked his beard thoughtfully. 'The process you describe is distillation. It purifies, condenses and extracts all the essential elements of the ingredients. The silver liquid will be an intensely powerful potion. But did she add any new ingredients before you boiled it?'

'Yes,' said Peter. 'I had to grind seeds.' He flexed his fingers as if the memory brought back the ache in his hands. 'Laburnum and foxglove. Then she added some yellow stuff beginning with S.'

'Sulphur,' suggested the wizard.

'Yes, that's it,' said Peter.

'And I had to collect the silver liquid in glass bottles,' said James.

'Now we are getting somewhere,' said the wizard. 'Tomorrow should bring us closer to our goal, but Emily, what is wrong? You do not seem pleased.'

'Oh! I'm glad about the spell, but Ammonia hates her dress. She says we have to start again but there isn't any material left and we're running out of time. I don't know what I'm going to do.'

'Ammonia will realize that the time has come for compromise. The Festival will take place in ten days time. There are only nine working days left. Look into her eyes and tell her what you have told me. I think you will convince her to accept the dress.'

'Hey ho! The Merry-O,' sang Ammonia as she led them down the spiralator on the following morning. 'I'm as happy as can be.' Today I'll test the spell. It will be wonderful and we'll celebrate with ice cream. But you must cheer up, come on, sing along with me. Hey ho! The Merry-O.'

The children joined in, subdued at first, but louder and louder as Ammonia pushed and prodded them into action.

'I'm as happy…' Her singing stopped abruptly when she caught sight of the dress. 'Curses,' she said as she turned on Emily. 'You've spoiled my day. What are you going to do about it?'

Remembering the wizard's words, Emily faced Ammonia and answered boldly. 'Nothing.'

'What?' Ammonia grabbed Emily by the chin. She tilted her head and bent down to look into Emily's eyes. 'Say that again if you dare.'

'Nothing,' Emily repeated. She winced as the witch's grip tightened but she didn't back down. 'I can't make another dress because there isn't any material, and even if there was, there isn't time. We only have nine days left, and that includes today.'

'Only nine?' Ammonia gasped and let go of Emily's chin. 'We had five weeks. Where have they gone?'

191

Emily shrugged. 'In working hard. In making the dress. I'm sorry you don't like it.'

'But I do like it,' said Ammonia. 'That's the trouble. I love it. It's fabulous. It's just the thought of wearing pink that freaks me out. I'm scared it'll stop me from being a witch.'

'But it didn't before,' said Emily. 'All those years of wearing pink didn't stop you, so why should it stop you now? Anyway, you could change the colour by magic.'

'Impossible,' said Ammonia. 'I told you, if there's the slightest smidgeon of magic, Mandragora or Vitriola will undo it and I'll be a laughing stock.'

She groaned, picked up the dress and examined the finished parts. 'It looks as if you've won again. I can't see any pink and if there isn't an alternative I suppose I'll have to wear it. But woe betides you if I see the smallest speck of pink.'

Emily returned to the sewing gang with both thumbs in the air and a triumphant smile. She settled down to sew, but she glanced round after almost every stitch. Something important was going to happen and she was determined not to miss it.

For an hour or so, there was silence. Then Ammonia strode out of the laboratory. 'Spitfire,' she shouted. 'You've got ten minutes to find a mouse.'

She pressed the button on her bracelet and the cat disappeared. Ten minutes later she pressed the button again and Spitfire came hurtling back. He sauntered across to Ammonia with a tail dangling from the corner of his jaws. He dropped the mouse at the witch's feet where it lay, un-moving.

'Gather round,' she cried. 'Prepare to witness my spell.'

The children put down their work and drew close. James picked up the mouse by its tail and held it up for everyone to see. Ammonia plucked a whisker from it and dropped it into a bottle of silver liquid. She screwed on the lid and shook the bottle vigorously.

'Here we go,' she said. 'Watch the Miracle of Materialization.'

With a flourish, she opened the bottle and out burst a beam of silver light. It shone with such intensity that the room and everything in it seemed to be made of silver. They all gazed upwards as the beam broke into hundreds of smaller beams that swirled and sparkled as they rose. Up and up they went, twirling and twining, and just before they reached the ceiling, they gathered together in a silver ball that dropped like a stone. It crashed onto the table and broke into a thousand fragments that scattered, faded and disappeared.

Ammonia's face grew pale. She tottered, sat down and stared at the place where the ball had landed. 'Where is it? It must be here.' Her voice rose to a shout. 'Don't just stand there, find it.'

'We don't know what we're looking for,' said Emily.

'The mouse, of course.' Ammonia whirled round the room, tossing cushions aside and peering into gaps between the furniture. The children searched and Spitfire searched, but the only mouse they found was the dead one that Spitfire had caught. Eventually Ammonia gave up and sent them back to work. Deep in thought, she dropped into the chair by the fire and called for Emily and James.

'I don't understand,' she said. 'It should have worked. You're the clever ones. Tell me what went wrong.'

'But we don't know what was supposed to happen,' said Emily.

'It should have turned into a mouse,' said Ammonia with growing impatience, 'a live mouse just like the other one.'

'There's your answer,' said James. 'The other one was dead. I don't think even you could bring a dead thing back to life.'

Ammonia clapped her hands. 'That's it,' she said. 'Spitfire, bring me a mouse, and this time I want it alive.'

Once again, Spitfire was sent through the fortress wall, and when he returned, the thing that dangled from his mouth struggled, squeaked and thrashed its long tail.

'That's a rat!' shrieked Ammonia. 'I'll get you for this, you stupid cat. I said a mouse. I can't abide rats. Don't you know the difference?'

Spitfire opened his mouth to answer. In a flash the rat was off. It scampered across the floor, brushed against Ammonia's boot and disappeared.

Ammonia scrambled onto a chair and held up her long skirt. 'Catch it,' she yelled, 'don't just stand there. Catch it.'

But there was no need for Emily or James to do anything. Spitfire pounced on the rat and carried it, still struggling and squealing, towards Ammonia.

'Stop,' she yelled. 'Don't bring it any closer. James you'll have to do it.'

James looked bewildered. 'Do what?'

'Get some hair,' she screamed.' Pull it out by the roots and bring it here.'

James went cautiously towards Spitfire. With finger and thumb he pulled a clump of fur from the part of the rat that was sticking out of Spitfire's mouth.

Ammonia, still teetering on the chair cried out. 'Kill it, Spitfire, kill it. I'm not getting down until it's dead.'

Chapter 37

With one jerk of Spitfire's head the rat lay still. Ammonia climbed down from the chair and told James to put the rat's hair in a bottle.

'Give it a shake and then open it,' she said.

As the beam of silver light burst from the bottle, her mouth opened wide in horror. 'Reverse the spell,' she cried. 'Reverse the spell. I forgot it was a rat!' But the beam had already split into smaller beams and although she tried to stop them, they kept on rising.

'Spitfire,' she screamed as she covered her face with her cloak. 'Catch it when it comes down. Kill it and tell me when it's gone.'

Up near the ceiling, the beams of light gathered together, not in one ball, but in a score or more. They didn't drop heavily as if they were dead. Like bubbles they drifted slowly down, swaying gently, this way and that. As the first one touched the lampshade it turned into a rat, a rat that scrabbled to cling on before falling to the floor. Spitfire pounced and laid its dead body in front of Ammonia.

'Got it,' he growled. 'You can come out now.'

Ammonia had only just uncovered her face when she screamed and covered it again. All around her, silver balls were landing, turning into rats, each one a clone of the one that Spitfire had caught. He ran around in a killing spree, littering the floor with dead bodies. Still they came, rats without number, scuttling and squeaking.

Ammonia went on screaming. The children's faces creased into smiles. They clamped their lips together and tried to suppress their laughter. Justin couldn't stop himself. He rolled on the floor behind the sofa and laughed until he cried.

'Hush,' Emily whispered as Spitfire sat down. 'I think that's the last one. Don't let Ammonia hear you laughing.'

The warning came just in time, for Ammonia stopped screaming and turned to James. Now that her fear had faded she was shaking with anger. 'You stupid boy. I'll eliminate you for this.'

'Strike,' Emily shouted.

Immediately the children gathered round James.

'Not again,' Ammonia shouted. 'I'll elim...'

'No,' Emily interrupted. 'You need James. Leave him alone and we'll go straight back to work. Anyway, he's discovered something amazing about your spell. You ought to thank him.'

The witch's head jerked up. 'Thank him! What for?'

Peter, clinging to his brother's arm explained. 'One hair, one rat, lots of hairs, lots of rats. That means you can make as many animals as you want.'

'Exactly,' said Emily. 'You could fill the stage with dozens of ra... I mean rabbits.'

Ammonia's eyes glistened. 'Rabbits!' She laughed uproariously. 'I'm going to get something better than rabbits.'

'But lunch is ready,' said Ben.

'Then eat it and get back to work,' she snapped. 'Spitfire, mind they behave. I won't be long.'

Chortling with glee she disappeared through the wall. Spitfire, who had tired himself out with rat-catching fell asleep. There was no one to watch them and they enjoyed their lunch without rushing. They talked in whispers, they laughed at the memory of

Ammonia surrounded by rats, and they asked if they could have pudding.

'Sure,' said Lisa, 'it's ice cream for everyone.'

The afternoon passed quietly and the evening meal was over by the time Ammonia returned. She hurtled through the wall and rushed round checking what they'd done in her absence.

'Not bad,' she said as she picked up a snake that Justin had made, 'but I want glittery eyes and a forked tongue. You can do it tomorrow. Go to bed now. I want to test my spell in peace.'

As soon as they were safely in their room and the wizard had appeared in his true form, Emily told their news.

'I thought it had something to do with hair,' she said.

'Rat's hair,' Peter chortled at the memory.

'Then she went out,' said James, 'and she came back with a bag full of something. I think it's different sorts of hair.'

'She'll turn it into animals,' said Peter. 'It's called the Miracle of Materialization.'

'Yes,' said James, 'and she can clone them. One hair, one animal, two hairs, two animals, but why does she wants them?'

A dreadful feeling of nausea washed over Emily. She swallowed and coughed before she managed to speak. 'Animals are just for practice,' she said. 'It's the hair in her locket that's important.'

The wizard held up his hand to stop her. 'I must communicate with my colleagues immediately. Suddenly her purpose is terrifyingly clear. This is a matter of extreme urgency.'

By the time the wizard lowered his hands the other children were asleep. Emily, tired though she was, had to replace the wizard's collar before she could sleep. She lay down, worrying about the hair in the locket and the person who had lost it.

'Now I know what the spell is for,' she said. 'It's about retribution. Ammonia's going to use the hair from her locket to materialize someone, and then she's going to punish…'

'Stop,' said the wizard, 'the less you know the safer you will be. You have challenged Ammonia and you have kept everyone safe. I know that your mind is filled with anxiety and I will make sure that you rest well tonight. As soon as you fasten my collar, you will sleep. But before that, I must give you instructions for the day of the Festival. I will try to tell you again, but in case something prevents me, please listen carefully. When Ammonia leaves I must follow. My colleagues will be waiting for me. When Ammonia passes through the wall their combined power will keep the portal open. It is my only chance and I must take it.'

Emily gasped and clutched her chest. 'Don't say that,' she begged. 'We need you here.'

'I'm sorry, but my place is with my fellow wizards. I must go with them for all our combined strength will be needed to counteract Ammonia's spell.'

'But if you can leave, why can't you take us with you?'

'Because you must stay here to release the other children.'

'But we don't know how to get into the room.'

'I will send someone to help you. '

'But you said all the wizards would be at the Festival.'

'This person is not a wizard. She possesses a special gift which, hopefully, will allow her to enter the fortress.'

Emily's voice rose in a panic. 'Only hopefully? What if she can't? What happens then?'

'I do not know, but I promise on my life that unless something unspeakable befalls me, I will come back. If anything prevents me, the other wizards will come.'

'But what if something happens to them?'

The wizard looked grave. 'I cannot tell a lie. I do not know.'

'So everything we've done could be for nothing?'

'I wish with all my heart that I could say otherwise, but I must be truthful. We can but hope for the best. Now, put on my collar and let us sleep.'

The last few days before the Festival passed in a whirl of activity. Ammonia examined her costume carefully. No pink was visible on the dress. The hat was wreathed in snakes with diamante eyes that reflected the light. The cloak shone with hundreds of stars and sequins. She looked round at the children, raised her finger and laughed maliciously.

'You've done a good job, but guess what? I don't need you any more.'

The children rushed to hide, flinging themselves behind the sofa, cowering under the table, disappearing into the kitchen. Only Emily faced the witch. Sounding far calmer than she felt, she pointed to the clock.

'Look at the time. You said you had to leave at four o'clock and it's already ten past. If you're late you'll be disqualified. You'd better go. You can decide what to do with us when you get back.'

Ammonia checked her watch. 'Toad spawn and pig's whiskers,' she cursed. 'You're right, but just you wait. I'll show you whether I need you or not.' With another burst of wild laughter she disappeared through the wall.

Ben had already been told what to do. He threw himself on top of Spitfire. Emily grabbed the cat's head and James unbuckled the collar. The tabby cat flashed before their eyes. The wizard appeared for no more than a second and then he followed Ammonia through the wall.

Part Three

Chapter 38

Startled from sleep by a voice calling her name, Merryn checked the time. It was not yet two o'clock but the voice was insistent.

'Merryn MacQueen. Go to Gylen Castle.'

She leapt out of bed, but halfway through dressing she stopped and stared at the carved wooden box. The voice that came out of it wasn't the usual voice. It was the voice of a woman. A terrifying thought grew in her head. What if the witch had broken into the wizards' communication system and was trying to trick her?

'Merryn, believe me,' said the voice. 'You and The Gift are needed immediately.'

'But how can I trust you when I don't know who you are?' Merryn demanded. 'Tobias told me not to go to the castle. If he's changed his mind he should tell me himself.'

'He would, if he could,' the voice replied. 'I am his wife and he instructed me to tell you that you are needed at the castle.'

Merryn was confused. If The Gift was needed it was her duty to go, but she had to be sure that she wasn't being drawn into a trap.

'I'm not going anywhere,' she decided, 'not until I speak to Tobias.'

'That is impossible. I repeat, Tobias is engaged in serious business and you are needed at the castle.'

Merryn started to undress. 'I'm going back to bed. I don't believe you.'

Other voices, women's voices rose in argument. Merryn held the box to her ear. She could make no sense of the jumbled words, but as she listened, a familiar voice rose above the rest

'Merryn.'

'Kester,' she gasped. 'Tell me this isn't a trick.'

'It is not a trick. The witch has left Gylen to attend the Festival of Malevolent Witches. Tobias and the other wizards have followed. Their combined power is needed to counteract a dangerous spell. Our future is at stake. Take your crystal and go to the castle.'

'But...'

Kester ignored her interruption. 'Hamish must take his crystal too. When you arrive at the doorway hold his hand and count slowly and clearly. On the count of seven you must jump over the threshold. Do not let go of his hand until you are inside. Now make haste for there are children in the fortress. One of them is a girl called Emily. She will show you what to do.'

Merryn's tummy turned over at the thought of imprisoned children, but she didn't want to become one of them.

'What if she captures us?' she asked.

'She is not there, that is why you must go now.'

There was a click followed by silence. Merryn pulled on her clothes, but not quickly enough for the necklace of sea-beans and hag-stones. As if to remind her of the urgency of the task it began to bang against her collarbone.

'All right,' she snapped. 'There's no need to hurt me. I'm going.'

Hurriedly, she fastened her trainers and packed a torch, a first aid kit, a notebook and pencil in her

206

rucksack. She crossed the landing to Hamish's room and tried to pull him out of bed. 'Get up,' she whispered. 'We have to go to the castle.'

Hamish merely grunted.

She grabbed his shoulders and shook him. 'Kester says we have to go to the castle and you have to bring your crystal.'

At the mention of Kester's name, Hamish leapt up. He dressed quickly and took his crystal from a drawer. 'I don't know why I need it though,' he said. 'It's nothing but a keepsake now.'

Nevertheless, he slipped it into his pocket and a few minutes later they were heading towards the castle on their mountain bikes.

'But what do we have to do?' Hamish asked as they rode along.

'Rescue a girl called Emily.'

'You mean the witch has a prisoner?' Hamish pulled on his brakes, screeched to a halt and shouted after her. 'I'm not coming. She might catch me.'

Merryn called over her shoulder. 'Don't be selfish. If you were trapped you'd want someone to rescue you, and the witch won't catch you because she isn't there. That's why we have to go now. Anyway, Kester said you had to come, so you'd better do as he says.'

Hamish got back on his bike. 'OK,' he said, 'but I'm not coming for you. I'm coming for Kester.'

As they rode on, it was not Gylen Castle, but the witch's fortress that Merryn saw. The shock of seeing it towering high into the sky made her lose her balance. She almost fell off her bike and had to put one foot down to steady herself. Immediately, the necklace jolted, reminding her that she must go on. She made her way to the foot of the castle mound. There she left her bike, and with Hamish close behind her, she scrambled up towards the forbidding walls.

'It's no use. I can't see the real castle.' She peered through half-closed eyes. 'We have to jump through the doorway and I don't know where it is.'

'That's why you need me,' said Hamish. 'Here, hold my hand and I'll lead you to the top step.'

It was a strange experience for Merryn, feeling her way down stairs that she couldn't see, but soon they were safely at the bottom.

'This is it,' said Hamish, 'we're on the doorstep.'

'Now we have to count,' said Merryn, 'and when we reach seven we have to jump inside.' She gripped his hand tightly. 'Start counting now: one, two, three, four, five, six, seven.'

On the count of seven, pulling Hamish along with her, she leapt over the threshold.

'Crumbs,' said Hamish. 'It doesn't look like a ruined castle to me.'

'It isn't,' said Merryn. 'It's the witch's fortress. We're inside and now we have to find Emily.'

'That's me,' said a girl as she crawled out from under the table, 'and this is James.'

'You scared us to death,' said James. 'We thought Ammonia was back.'

'Ammonia!' Hamish exclaimed. 'What sort of a name is that?'

'The witch's name,' said Emily, 'but there isn't time to explain. We have to rescue the others before she comes back.'

'Others,' Merryn gasped.

As she spoke, a group of boys and girls stepped out from behind the sofa.

'Crumbs,' said Hamish as he counted them. 'Why did she want ten children?'

'To work,' said Emily, 'but that's not all. Prepare yourselves for a shock.'

'I've had a shock already,' said James. 'Spitfire said he'd send someone to help, but we didn't expect a couple of kids. I don't see what they can do.'

'Wait,' said Emily. 'They got inside. So they must know some magic.'

James shrugged as if he was unconvinced.

Hamish scowled. 'My sister has magical powers and you'd better believe it.'

Merryn nudged him with her elbow. 'No need for that,' she said. 'I can do things that ordinary mortals can't do, but I'm not here to take charge.' She looked anxiously at Emily. 'Tobias said you'd tell me what to do.'

'I thought you'd tell us,' said Emily, 'but we have a plan and if you can open the door it should work.' She pointed to the spray bottles filled with green liquid. 'Come on, everyone. Grab a couple of those and follow me.'

She picked up a walking stick and banged the floor in the corner of the room. There was a rumbling sound as a section of shelves slid away to reveal a door.

'It's locked,' she said, 'and Ammonia took the keys, so unless you can open it, we're stuck.'

James turned to Merryn. 'If you really do have magical powers you'd better start using them.'

'Merryn held the crystal and murmured to Hamish. 'If this doesn't work I don't know what will.'

209

Hamish gave her a push. 'Touch the keyhole,' he urged. 'Go on, hurry up.'

She looked at the expectant faces. James wrinkled his nose and shook his head as if he had no faith at all. Emily held her breath. The other children crossed their fingers.

Conscious of eleven pairs of eyes watching her, Merryn stepped towards the door. If it opened, they stood a chance, but if it didn't – what then?

Chapter 39

As the door swung open Emily and James rushed inside. Merryn hesitated as a dreadful stench filled her lungs. She peered into the gloom, looking for captive children, but all she could see were rows of cages. They filled the room, stretching as far as her eyes could see. Whatever she'd expected, it wasn't this.

'Crumbs,' said Hamish. 'It's a blooming zoo.'

'Except they're not animals.' said Emily. Her voice shook as she added, 'They're children, at least they were once.'

Hamish gasped. He turned his head away and retched.

Merryn staggered backwards. There wasn't a word to express the nausea that threatened to swamp her. She pulled herself together, took a tentative step towards the first cage and opened it.

'But,' she said, 'it's empty.'

'No,' said Emily as she pulled out a stick insect. 'It's really a boy. Watch this. We can reverse the transformation.'

As she sprayed the green liquid the stick insect disappeared under a heap of bubbles. A sudden explosion sent lumps of foam flying in every direction and the air filled with evil green mist. For one brief moment Merryn glimpsed a tall, gangly boy, but before she had time to speak, he vanished.

'Crumbs,' said Hamish again. 'If that's rescuing someone I hope you never have to rescue me.'

'But where is he?' Merryn demanded. 'What's happened to him?'

'He's fine,' said Emily. 'He's gone home.'

'But how can you be sure?' Hamish asked.

'Ammonia told us,' said James, 'and Spitfire checked. He's really a wizard but he changed himself into a cat so that he could spy on Ammonia.'

Merryn gasped. 'So that's what Tobias did.'

Emily looked at her expectantly. 'What do you mean?'

'Not now,' James interrupted. He raised his voice and shouted. 'Listen everyone, we'll change you back into your true selves and send you home. Come out, so that we can help you.' He turned to the others. 'Lift them out and get spraying.'

As his voice died away, there came the sound of rustling straw. It grew in intensity as all kinds of creatures emerged from hiding. Merryn opened a cage and balked at the sight of a huge spider.

'Read the label,' Emily urged. 'It's Janie Morrison. Don't think about what she is now. Think about what she should be.'

Tentatively Merryn put her hand inside the cage. The spider moved towards her on its eight hairy legs. She cringed as it climbed onto her fingers. Instinctively she pulled her hand away and the spider fell to the floor.

In one quick movement James pushed her aside and aimed the spray. The green liquid bubbled, foamed and exploded. A girl with a mass of black curls flashed before Merryn's eyes and was gone.

James turned on her angrily. 'You stupid thing. You could have injured her.'

'I'm sorry,' Merryn stammered. 'It won't happen again.'

'It had better not,' James retorted, 'or you might as well go back where you came from.'

After that cutting rebuke, Merryn steeled herself. She lifted out all manner of insects. Each one was sprayed and each one disappeared. The other children rushed round, lifting out creatures, spraying them and moving on. Still the cages stretched into the distance. Each explosion released more mist. It rose in clouds to hang in a pall over the room.

Soon the spray bottles were empty. James brought replacements and the spraying went on. Halfway down the room the creatures changed. Now there were frogs, toads, slugs, snails, lizards and snakes. They too were sprayed. A carpet of foam grew until it lay ankle deep on the floor. The mist grew thicker, so thick that it was difficult to see, but still they went on. Again the spray bottles were emptied.

James came back with another armful. 'These are the last,' he said as he handed them round. 'Let's hope there's enough.'

Next they found mice and rabbits. As soon as their cages were opened, they leapt out and sat on their haunches, their whiskers twitching as they waited to be sprayed. When the last one had disappeared they came to the pigs. Emily shook her empty bottle. The others did the same. They looked at one another in dismay.

'I can't bear it.' Emily choked on her words. 'We promised to save them and we can't.'

The pigs began to squeal. They hurled themselves at the walls of their pens and looked at the children with desperation in their eyes.

'Let them out,' said Hamish. 'If they roll in the foam it might work.'

Quickly they ran from pen to pen, pulling back bolts and standing aside as the pigs dashed out

'Roll in it,' shouted James. 'It's your only chance.'

The pigs lay down and kicked their legs in the air. They rolled about, but nothing happened.

'They're not getting covered properly,' said Merryn. 'We've got to help them.' She picked up a handful of foam and spread it over the nearest pig. When every speck of pink was covered, there was an enormous explosion. She caught a momentary glimpse of a boy, and then he too disappeared.

'It worked!' Emily shouted. 'Thank goodness it worked.'

The pigs stood quietly, their bodies dappled pink and green. Working frantically, the children smeared them with foam. Explosion after explosion crackled like gunfire. Gobbets of foam were flung high into the air. As each lump fell, every bench, every cage and every surface was hidden from view, and the last pig vanished. The twelve children stood in silence, listening for any movement, making sure that there was no one left to rescue.

'We've done it,' said Emily. 'Now let's get rid of this awful stuff. I wish there was a shower, but all we've got is a sink.'

'This might help.' Merryn held up the crystal. As its pink rays spread through the room the foam slowly disappeared.

'Wow!' said James. 'Where did you get that?'

'It's a long story,' said Merryn. 'I'll tell you when we're safely out of here. Come on, show me which way to go.'

Emily's face turned pale. 'You mean you don't know?'

'We've no idea,' said Merryn. 'Tobias said you'd tell us what to do. We thought you'd know.'

'Don't be stupid,' said James. 'If we knew how to get out we'd have gone long ago.'

Hamish groaned. 'If we're still here when the witch gets back...' His words tailed away. He flopped down and buried his head in his hands.

Merryn let the rays of the pink crystal sweep round the room, but she couldn't find a door. She walked round again, trying to find a chink that would open to the outside world. There was nothing. She slumped in the chair next to Hamish. Her eyes met Emily's and she shook her head helplessly.

'I can't find a way out,' she whispered. 'We're trapped.'

'I refuse to be trapped,' said James. He picked up Ammonia's stick and went round the room whacking shelves and cupboards. It was no use. Nothing moved and he too gave up the search and sat down.

'Maybe we can break through like Ammonia did,' said Ben. He took a run and hurled himself at the wall.

The others gasped as Ben fell back with blood pouring from his nose.

'He's knocked himself out,' said Merryn as she knelt down and placed her crystal on his forehead.

Emily brought water and a cloth to clean away the blood. 'It's a pity it didn't work,' she said. 'It was really brave of him to try. I hope he's going to be OK. We can't get a doctor or…anything. It's hopeless.'

They stood helplessly until Ben eventually stirred. He put his hand to his head and sat up unsteadily.

'Sorry,' he gave a rueful grin. 'I feel awful but it was worth a try. Come on, we can't give up. We've got to think of something.'

Chapter 40

Across the sea, on a hill above the town of Oban, Ammonia stepped through the archway of McCaig's Tower. Unknown to the people who lived in the town she was entering one of the meeting places of the Association of Malevolent Witchery. She looked up at the spectacular crystal dome and gazed round at tier upon tier of black velvet seats. Her eyes lit up when she saw the stage where she would demonstrate her mastery of magic. She'd arrived! This was the culmination of four hundred and ninety nine years of hard work. She would show them what a real witch could do! Pride and confidence surged through her as she went backstage to find her dressing room.

'My time has come,' she said as she closed the door. 'Before this night ends I will sit on the thirteenth chair.'

Grinning gleefully she put on the dress and stepped back to admire the coloured squares. 'Thank you mother,' she laughed, 'your dresses came in useful after all. If you could see me now you'd die all over again.'

For a moment she reflected on her promise to send Emily home. 'Hah! So much for promises.' She shook her head decisively. 'There's no way I'm keeping that promise. I'll eliminate the others but I'll keep her. She can be my wardrobe mistress and I'll be the best dressed witch of all time.'

She fastened the cloak with its silver lining and placed the hat on her head and looked in the mirror. The snakes coiled round her head, their jewel eyes reflecting the light, their forked tongues poking out threateningly. Briefly, she wondered if she'd gone too far. The snake was the symbol of The Grand High Witch and here she was wearing a dozen or more, but she shrugged the feeling away.

'See if I care,' she said to her reflection. 'I'm as good as her and when I perform my spell they'll understand.'

She had just unpacked her jars and placed them on a silver tray when a voice boomed out. 'Attention! Contestants must immediately present themselves to the stage manager.'

With sudden misgivings she removed the hat. Then, covering her costume with her old cloak, she strode along the corridor to where the other two witches were waiting. She gave a malicious chuckle when she saw that Vitriola was huddled in a corner as if she was afraid to say boo to a goose. But when she turned to the other witch her heart sank. Mandragora Twitch was looking glamorous and confident.

Mandragora looked Ammonia up and down. 'Call that a costume,' she sneered, 'you haven't made much of an effort.' She stroked the fine spider's web of her gown and twirled around so that its dewdrops sparkled and shimmered. Then she curled her lip contemptuously and pushed onto the stage in front of Ammonia.

'Just you wait,' Ammonia muttered,' you'll get your comeuppance or I'm not a Clickfinger.'

Beyond the glare of footlights Ammonia could see nothing, but she didn't care. The audience was of no interest to her. She looked enviously at The Grand High Witch sitting on her throne. She looked at the other eleven members of The Grand High Council, but most of all she looked at the empty chair. That's what she'd come for – nothing else mattered.

The Grand High Witch rose to her feet. 'The winner of this contest,' she said, 'if she proves worthy, will win the thirteenth chair. The contestants will perform in the following order. Mandragora M Twitch, Vitriola P Sniff and Ammonia B Clickfinger. The last two contestants must return to their dressing rooms and remain there until they are called to perform.

Ammonia opened her mouth to protest. 'But...'

She swallowed her words as The Grand High Witch glared. 'If you wish to perform you must leave the stage immediately. Contestants are not allowed to observe their competitors.'

'But...' Ammonia began.

The Grand High Witch rose to her feet. 'You forget yourself,' she roared. 'Another word and you will be banned from the contest.'

Spitting with indignation Ammonia returned to her dressing room. Furiously she slammed the door. All her plans for scuppering the other acts had been a waste of time. Or had they? If only she could see what was happening on the stage, she might be able to spoil the spells and make her rivals look incompetent. She clicked her finger at the wall, but her magic bounced back. She tried the door, but it had been locked. A scowl spread across her forehead. For the first time in her life, she was being forced to play fair.

The wait seemed interminable. She could hear nothing above an occasional roar of applause. The suspense played on her nerves. She paced up and down, twiddling the whiskers on her largest wart and willing Mandragora to fail. Eventually, a great cheering penetrated her room. It went on for a very long time. Ammonia fumed and ground her teeth. Mandragora had obviously pleased the audience.

As the sound died away, Vitriola was called to the stage. This time there was a long silence. Ammonia, unable to stop her pacing, listened anxiously for the cheering that would mark the end of the act. When it eventually came, it was more muted than before. Mingled with the clapping, there were boos and hisses. Vitriola had failed to impress. Now it appeared to be between her and Mandragora.

Back in the fortress, Merryn looked at the clock. The hands pointed to twenty past nine. 'Hang on,' she said, 'is that night or morning?'

'Night,' said Emily.'

'It can't be right,' said Merryn.

'It never is,' said Emily, 'but it's the time we live by. It's witch time. What time is it really?'

Merryn hadn't put on her watch. 'I don't know,' she said. 'We were called out of bed in the middle of the night. It was still dark when we arrived.'

'Yes,' said Hamish, 'and we missed breakfast. Is there anything to eat? I'm starving.'

'That's the only good thing about this place,' said Ben. 'You can have whatever you want. You can have pizza in twenty minutes.'

'Suits me,' said Hamish.'

The pizzas were cooked and eaten. Hours passed. The children were exhausted and overcome with despair. They'd tried everything to find a way out. James had whacked every single wall. Heather and Hazel had searched the laboratory. Peter, Megan and

Rosie had crawled all over the floors, banging and listening for hollow sounds that might lead to secret passages. Ben and Justin had tapped the ceilings with long sticks. Lisa and Emily had searched the kitchen, emptying cupboards and looking for spaces behind them. Merryn had done what the others couldn't do. She'd used her crystal to open locked drawers, and she and Hamish had searched the witch's private papers for a spell that would allow them to escape, but they couldn't find the leather-bound spell book anywhere. They'd even returned to the zoo to see if there was a way out from there. It was all to no avail.

'Contact Kester,' Hamish said. 'I know you were told not to, but it's our last chance. Do it. Please.'

'I already tried,' she said. 'It doesn't work. We're sealed in. There's a barrier round us. We can't get out and the messages can't get out either. We're trapped.'

Chapter 41

Ammonia was called to the stage. Wearing the hat and with her old cloak removed she picked up her tray and stepped into the spotlight. The Grand High Witch announced her act.

'Ammonia B Clickfinger will now present The Miracle of Materialisation. But wait.' She held up her hand and beckoned to Ammonia to come closer. 'What is the meaning of the hat? How dare you adorn yourself with snakes? It is a wonderful hat, but not for the likes of you. I will have it.'

Ammonia spluttered with indignation, but she daren't disobey. The Grand High Witch was waiting with her hand outstretched. The eleven witches of The Grand High Council had risen to their feet. The members of the audience were whispering excitedly.

Everyone was waiting to see what she would do. Reluctantly she removed the hat and The Grand High Witch snatched it and cradled it in her lap.

'Now you may begin,' said The Grand High Witch.

Shaken by such a bad start, Ammonia threw back her cloak to reveal her magnificent multi-coloured dress. There was a smattering of applause, but not enough to restore her confidence. With shaking hands she turned to the silver tray and opened the first jar. A ray of silver light broke into beams that swirled up to gather in a ball of iridescent beauty. Very slowly it floated down and as it touched the floor it burst open and a skylark hopped out. It huddled on the floor, its shoulders hunched, its head drawn into its neck.

'Is that all?' demanded The Grand High Witch.

Ammonia scowled at the skylark. 'Drat you,' she muttered. 'You're supposed to fly. You're supposed to sing.' She pushed her toe under the bird and kicked it into the air. It flew up and battered its wings against the dome, but it didn't sing.

'Enough,' said The Grand High Witch. 'We must have something better.'

Overcome with embarrassment, Ammonia clicked her finger at the skylark. As soon as it disappeared she opened the second jar. The beams of light rose up and formed a larger ball. Ammonia cringed when she saw where it was going to land. A Member of the Grand High Council yelled in panic as a vulture appeared on her shoulder. There was laughter from the audience, but the expression on the witch's face told Ammonia that she'd made an enemy. Quickly she clicked her finger and the vulture vanished.

The next jar produced two gibbons. Startled by the applause, they leapt into the air and proceeded to swing from light to light across the ceiling. The audience cheered, the gibbons swung faster. Ammonia tried to dispatch them, but they were travelling too fast. Each time she clicked her finger her magic missed and hit the dome with a resounding bang. The audience hooted with laughter. The Grand High Witch called a halt, but many minutes passed before Ammonia managed to dispatch the gibbons by catching them in mid-swing.

'Entertaining,' said The Grand High Witch, 'but not accomplished. It was a fiasco. If you cannot control your manifestations you would be wise to produce something less mobile.'

Delighted laughter followed her words. Anxiously Ammonia turned to the next jar. The hair inside was soft and furry. She hesitated, afraid of what might happen when the tiger appeared. She was right to be concerned for it arrived with a roar that chilled her to the bone. It came towards her, growling ferociously. She flung up her hand to magic it away, but she lost her balance and fell on her back. There was a gasp from the audience as the tiger leapt. Just in time, Ammonia clicked her finger and the tiger vanished. She struggled to her feet, caught her breath and paused to calm her nerves.

The Grand High Witch was not prepared to wait. 'Proceed immediately,' she insisted, 'or withdraw.'

'Never!' Ammonia retorted.

Nothing was going to plan. Why was her carefully rehearsed act changing in such unpredictable ways? Was it the lights, the other witches, or the noise that was affecting the animals so badly? Even though she was dreading what might happen, she opened the next jar. The beam of silver light rose, carrying with it a thick, bristly hair. It struggled to rise as if something was too heavy to carry. It grew into a gigantic ball that plummeted down and landed on the stage with a resounding crash. Out stepped an elephant. It swung its trunk, took the snake hat from The Grand High Witch's lap and gave it back to Ammonia. The audience went wild, but when it plucked the hat from The Grand High Witch's head the cheers turned to stunned silence.

'Remove the beast,' roared The Grand High Witch.

Ammonia knew that the hat was an ancient symbol of power, as important to The Grand High Witch as a crown is to a Queen. 'I can't,' she gasped. 'If I remove the elephant, the hat will go with it.'

The Grand High Witch roared even louder. 'Then remove the hat from the elephant.'

Ammonia tried to reach the hat, but the elephant swung its trunk into the air and placed the hat on its own head. Some members of the audience tittered. They hid their faces behind their hands, but The Grand High Witch had heard and her face turned red with fury. Silence fell. The witches waited, wondering what the elephant would do next. Time passed. Tension grew. The elephant plucked the hat from its own head and placed it on Ammonia's.

For a few glorious moments, Ammonia forgot the elephant. She felt the power of The Grand High Witch's hat. It gave her strength and confidence. She rose to her full height, convinced that this was her destiny. The audience hissed. The Grand High Witch marched across the stage and tore the hat from Ammonia's head.

'You trained it to give the hat to you,' she bellowed. 'How dare you insult me? How dare you insult our ancient symbol of power?'

Ammonia shook her head in bewildered denial. The elephant trumpeting loudly, reminded her of what she must do. With a click of her finger it was gone and she opened the next jar before The Grand High Witch returned to her seat.

This was risky. In a last minute flash of inspiration she'd put one of Emily's hairs into the jar. Working with animals was one thing, producing a human being would surely gain approval. Once again the silver rays rose up to the ceiling and formed into a ball. Just as

The Grand High Witch pointed an accusing finger at Ammonia, the ball floated down and landed on the table in front of her. Out popped Emily, balancing precariously, her hand clamped over her mouth, her eyes wide with shock. She jumped off the table and looked round for a place to hide. As she ran from one side of the stage to the other, the audience cheered and The Grand High Witch clapped her hands.

'You have redeemed yourself,' she said to Ammonia. 'Give her to me and I will forgive the incident with the hat.'

Before her words ended, Ammonia clicked her finger and Emily vanished.

'Bring her back immediately,' shouted the Grand High Witch. 'I want her.'

'I can't. I only had one...' Ammonia stopped as she realised she'd almost given away her secret.

'Explain yourself,' said The Grand High Witch.

'I mean,' stuttered Ammonia, 'that I only had enough in the jar for...'

'Enough what?' The Grand High Witch demanded.

Ammonia looked straight into her questioner's eyes. 'I refuse to say. It is my life's work. I will not share it.'

All the witches booed their disapproval, but The Grand High Witch raised her hand for silence.

'Your answer displeases me, but it is unreasonable to ask you to give your secrets to everyone. However, if you win the contest your spell must be shared with me, and I must have the girl. If you do not agree, you must leave the stage immediately.

'Do you accept my conditions?'

Chapter 42

Ammonia was afraid to give her spell away because some of her power would go with it. But if she refused, she wouldn't be allowed to produce The Great Wizard, and that was the whole purpose of her act. Reluctantly she nodded her head.

'Then you may continue,' said The Grand High Witch, 'but I will not tolerate any more insolence.'

Ammonia's confidence was in tatters, but if the final spell worked she was confident that she would win the contest. All the previous manifestations had led to this moment, and although they'd all proved unpredictable, this was likely to be the most unpredictable of all. She hadn't tested it because The Great Wizard was powerful enough to end her life the moment he appeared. Now, aided by the combined magic of all the witches, she was sure that her revenge would be complete.

'For the finale,' she said, 'I require the help of you all.' She sent a trumpet fanfare through the hall. When it ended she called at the top of her voice. 'My final manifestation will be The Great Wizard himself.'

The audience gasped in unison. The Grand High Witch's eyebrows rose so high that they disappeared under the brim of her hat. 'Impossible,' she murmured.

'Not so,' said Ammonia. 'When I give the signal, whatever your means of magic – wand or finger, breath or voice, use it. Together we can eliminate him and in so doing, Benevolent Wizardry will be in our power.'

There was fidgeting as some witches brought out their wands. Others raised their fingers while some prepared to sniff or blow, to twitch their noses or to call out their magic words. When every witch was ready, an expectant silence fell. Ammonia unscrewed the jar. The beam of light that emerged was so blinding that all the witches shielded their eyes from the unbearable glare.

Only Ammonia had protected her eyes for this moment. She watched the beam break into a million strands and she saw the long silver hair rise with them. She watched the strands form into a ball of such astounding beauty that it pierced her heart and made her gasp in pain. Only she was able to watch as it descended to the stage, but everyone saw what happened next. The ball shattered into myriads of silver shards and The Great Wizard stood before them.

Disappointed that the witches were not raising the roof with their cheers, Ammonia looked round. The reason was plain to see. Every mouth was open. Every witch was awestruck, staring at a sight they'd never expected to see. But despite their surprise they were ready to use their malevolent powers.

'Hah!' Ammonia laughed as she spoke to The Great Wizard. 'You are powerless. Now I will know the sweet taste of revenge. You are guilty of the murder of my father. Your punishment is death.'

The Grand High Witch, with The Snake Wand pointing at the prisoner, shouted at Ammonia. 'You forget yourself. Only I can pronounce the death penalty.'

'Then pronounce it,' Ammonia retorted. 'What are you waiting for?'

'Your rudeness is beyond belief,' said The Grand High Witch. 'I will pronounce it when I am ready, but first I must hear the prisoner's defence against the charge of murder. How do you plead?'

'Not guilty,' said The Great Wizard. 'I was victorious in fair and open combat.'

The Grand High Witch laughed. 'I believe you,' she said, 'but that fact will not save you. You are the enemy of Malevolent Witchery and you cannot be allowed to live. In a fair fight, one-to-one, you could destroy each and every one of us. You may even have the power to eliminate me, but that we will never know because now you are outnumbered.'

The Great Wizard bowed his head to accept the truth of the statement.

The Grand High Witch gave her order. 'On the count of three we must combine our powers to destroy him for ever.'

'No,' screamed Ammonia. 'It will only work for me. It's my spell. It's my revenge for the death of my father. I must give the order.'

'Nonsense.' The Grand High Witch bared her teeth and snarled. 'How dare you challenge me? I will give the order.'

Ammonia raised her voice to drown The Grand High Witch's words. 'I will give the order. Ready. Steady.'

The Grand High Witch joined in the count. Her voice rose above Ammonia's and when their combined voices reached three, all the witches released their destructive magic. What followed was pandemonium. The magic spells sped across the hall, but just before they reached the wizard, powerful forces intercepted them. Spells ricocheted and sped back to those who had sent them.

All the witches wailed or screamed in anguish. Ammonia's finger burst into flame. Howling with pain she tried to douse it. She wrapped it in a fold of her dress, she spat on it, she stuck it in her mouth and sucked it, but the flame would not die. It burned and burned until all that remained of her long black finger was a small, shrivelled stump.

'You failed,' yelled The Grand High Witch in a voice that was harsh with scorn. 'You have caused pain to your fellow witches, you have wrecked their wands, you have injured their fingers, you have burned their noses, their magic words have returned to choke them. You have insulted me and you have made a mockery of this prestigious occasion. And it was all in vain because your prisoner has disappeared.'

'That's impossible,' Ammonia stammered.

'I assure you it is true,' said The Grand High Witch. 'You have failed miserably and very soon we will decide your fate, but first I call on the other two contestants to join us.'

At her command Mandragora and Vitriola walked onto the stage and took their places next to Ammonia.

'Now we must decide if one of them is worthy of the thirteenth chair,' she continued. 'The final decision is mine, but you may all express an opinion. Think carefully before you speak. Is Ammonia worthy of that honour?'

'No.' The unanimous reply was accompanied by boos, hisses and the stamping of feet. Ammonia knew that her dream of revenge had shattered. Her legs gave way. She slumped to the floor and the audience broke into gales of derisive laughter.

'And what of Vitriola?'

'No,' was the unenthusiastic reply.

'I agree,' said The Grand High Witch. 'She has much to learn and must apply herself more diligently, but we will allow her another year so that she can perform at the next Festival.'

It looked as if Mandragora would win. Losing to a member of the Twitch family was more than Ammonia could bear. She struggled to her feet and spat at Mandragora.

'Apologise,' roared The Grand High Witch.

Ammonia refused. She'd failed, but she would take orders from no one.

'Then suffer the consequences,' said The Grand High Witch. She turned her back on Ammonia and asked. 'Shall we appoint Mandragora M Twitch?'

The witches couldn't agree.

Ammonia added her voice to those who were against. 'No,' she shouted, 'Never.'

The members of The Grand High Council huddled together and eventually The Grand High Witch spoke.

'Mandragora gave a creditable performance, but she is not quite ready to join The Council. However, she too is granted another year and we will expect her to improve her performance at the next Festival.

Ammonia grinned as Mandragora's face turned dark with disappointment. Forgetting her own predicament she punched the air and cheered.

The Grand High Witch waited until silence fell. 'I regret that the thirteenth chair will remain unfilled, but those of you who have aspirations may apply for the next contest. I hope then to find someone worthy of the honour.'

'I thought that would conclude the meeting,' she added, 'but now we must consider Ammonia B Clickfinger. Her spell failed. Apart from The Snake Wand she has damaged every means of making magic in this room. We must contemplate her punishment with the utmost care.'

Chapter 43

Back in the witch's fortress Emily's heart was pounding. She'd imagined herself face to face with The Grand High Witch. There'd been cheers and she'd been running, desperately searching for a way to escape. She looked round and shook the feeling away when she saw that nothing had changed. The other children lay, clinging together, catching up on sleep after the long working days of the last few weeks. They were still trapped and there was nothing they could do about it. If she hadn't insisted on more helpers they would have been home by now. Instead she'd placed them in even greater danger. She felt sorry and stupid and angry and helpless all at the same time.

A sudden beeping broke into her thoughts. At last, something was going to happen. 'It's Spitfire's collar,' she said. 'Ammonia's calling him and she'll go bananas if it arrives without him.'

James ran to the table and caught hold of the buckle. He hung on with all his strength but it struggled as if it was alive. Peter ran to help but even though he hung on too, it broke away and shot through the wall.

'She'll come back,' Emily gasped, her face turning pale. 'She'll know something's wrong.'

'She won't,' said James. 'I bet she's still on the stage.' He grinned and slapped Peter on the back. 'Something's gone wrong with her act.'

Emily turned to Merryn. 'I think he's right. She'd never leave us without a guard.'

'Witchvision!' James exclaimed as he leapt to his feet. 'Why didn't I think of it before? Ammonia said they'd televise the contest. I'm going to switch on.'

Emily grabbed his arm and tried to stop him. 'Don't. Ammonia said we'd get a shock if we ever touched it.'

James struggled to free himself but Emily wouldn't let go. She screamed at him and he shouted back.

Merryn pushed her way between them. 'Stop it,' she yelled. 'Falling out won't help. We need to think carefully and then take a vote. Let's look at the facts. We're trapped and when Ammonia comes back she'll know we've been plotting against her.'

'She'll punish us anyway,' said Ben. 'So we might as well risk it.'

'I vote we switch on,' said James. 'I'm fed up of wondering what's happening. I'd rather know.'

'So would I,' said Merryn. 'Hands up for switching on.'

James counted. 'Nine for,' he said, 'and three against. I'm sorry, Emily, but you're outnumbered.'

Emily backed away as if she expected the set to explode. She sat on the floor behind the sofa. 'If it's a booby trap this could be the end of us,' she said. 'So if you're going to do it, make it quick. I can't stand the suspense.'

James stood with his hand on the button. 'Well, if it does explode it might make a hole in the wall and then we can get out. It can't be worse than being trapped. Duck for cover everyone.'

Within seconds, they had all disappeared. James switched on and dived under the table. For a whole minute nothing happened, then there was a crackling sound and a picture began to appear. 'See,' he said, 'it's absolutely fine. She was bluffing.'

'Look at Ammonia,' said Emily as she peered over the sofa. 'She's hanging on to the table. She looks as if she's going to fall over.'

'Look at the other one,' said James. 'I think she's in charge.'

'She must be The Grand High Witch,' said Merryn, 'and she's pointing her wand at Ammonia.'

'It's like a snake,' said Hamish. 'It's got eyes and a forked tongue. Crumbs, it isn't like a snake. It is a snake! A snake wand, how cool is that?'

'Shush,' said James. 'She's saying something.'

As they watched, Spitfire's collar burst through the crystal dome. Emily held her breath, wondering what Ammonia would do when she saw that it had arrived without Spitfire. The camera followed the collar as it whirled round the room and came to rest on the stage. At the sight of it Ammonia lost control.

'Spitfire,' she screamed as she clutched the collar. 'Where are you? I've been betrayed. There was nothing wrong with my spell. It was those...'

The Grand High Witch cut her off with a snarl. 'There seems to be no end to your stupidity. On top of everything else you have damaged the dome. I give no further warning. One more stupid act and I'll silence you for ever.'

'Yes!' Hamish jumped to his feet and punched the air. 'Go on, do it.'

But The Grand High Witch did not do it. Ammonia stuffed her fist in her mouth as if she was trying to stifle the strangled moans that rose from her throat.

The Grand High Witch addressed the audience. 'Without further delay we must consider the sentence on Ammonia B Clickfinger. Think carefully. Do not let your emotions run away with you. Consider all the options and in half an hour we will reconvene to make our decision. In the meantime I will ensure that our captive does not escape.'

Ammonia, clutching Spitfire's collar started to run. But The Snake Wand caught her in mid-stride and rooted her to the spot. The camera focused on her, and her picture remained on the screen while the other witches withdrew from the hall.

'It's the Stun-Dumb spell,' said Emily. It's what she did to me.'

'And me, said Rosie.'

'Me too,' said Megan. 'Now she knows what it feels like.'

James pointed and began to giggle. He rolled back on the sofa, clutching his chest and breaking into gales of laughter. The others joined in. Every time they stopped, one of them pointed to Ammonia, and the laughter started again. They laughed until tears rolled down their cheeks. They laughed until Merryn stood in front of the Witchvision screen and yelled at them to stop.

'It might be funny. It certainly serves her right but I don't see what there is to laugh about. Have you forgotten that we're still trapped?'

James tried to stifle his laughter. 'Sorry,' he said, 'but it feels good to laugh after all we've been through.'

A fanfare of trumpets made them turn again to the screen. The picture changed. The witches were returning. They were pushing and shoving, jostling one another as they tried to reach the front seats. The Grand High Witch and members of The Grand High Council took their places. Ammonia, still immobile, looked like a model of a character from a ghastly horror movie.

'Crumbs,' said Hamish. 'How many witches are there?'

'Too many,' said Merryn 'How will we ever get rid of them all?'

The Grand High Witch pointed The Snake Wand at Ammonia and the spell that held her was broken. She wobbled and only just managed to regain her balance. Then she looked round as if she'd forgotten where she was.

Chapter 44

Ammonia had turned a ghastly shade of green. She was badly shaken, but she was determined not to fall. She clutched the edge of the table and hung on for all she was worth. Her mind raced over and over the failure of her magic. It had been sabotaged. That was certain. She was powerful, that was without question, but she knew her limitations. She was not powerful enough to cause so much harm to her fellow witches.

'It wasn't me,' she yelled. 'It…'

'Silence,' The Grand High Witch commanded.

Now she understood what had really happened, Ammonia couldn't stop. Under her breath she went on grumbling. 'The Benevolent Wizards damaged your magic. Those pesky brats and the dratted cat betrayed me. When I get hold of them they'll wish they'd never been born.'

The Grand High Witch turned away from Ammonia and addressed the audience. 'Despite her ill manners,' she said, 'I have decided that Ammonia B Clickfinger deserves another chance.'

The audience erupted in a roar of disapproval. The spotlight turned on Ammonia as she raised one arm in triumph. Witches rose to their feet, stamping, booing and hissing their displeasure.

'Although her spell failed,' The Grand High Witch continued, 'it was remarkable. A witch who can materialise The Great Wizard is too valuable to lose.'

Ammonia raised her head and grinned. Her spell had been praised. She looked across at the empty chair and her spirits lifted. Soon it would be hers.

There were more boos and hisses from the audience. The Grand High Witch called for silence. 'If her spell had not been reversed she would have rendered the most significant service to Malevolent Witchery. Her punishment will be one year's banishment from The Association of Malevolent Witches. During that time she must re-work her spell. If she can produce The Great Wizard at our next Festival she will be forgiven.'

'That means she can come back,' Emily shrieked. 'She can go on being a witch. She'll be back any minute and she'll...'

'Hush,' said Merryn. 'I don't think that's the end of it. There's going to be trouble. Look, the witches are really angry.'

From somewhere in the audience, a voice called out, 'It's not enough. Eliminate, eliminate.'

'Eliminate, eliminate.' More and more voices joined the chant.

The Grand High Witch pointed The Snake Wand at the audience but the chant went on. The words swelled until Ammonia fell on her knees and covered her ears. Some witches rose to their feet. They jostled one another and pushed their way towards the stage. Others kept up the chant, stamping their feet until the whole building vibrated to the rhythm. The Grand High Witch drew her Council into a corner, and still the witches advanced. Soon, the first ones had reached the steps that led onto the stage.

The Grand High Witch turned and bellowed. 'I have taken your feelings into account but we need a witch who can produce The Great Wizard. Is anyone else able to do that? Raise your hand if you can. Otherwise, return to your seats.'

The witches stopped advancing. They fell silent. They looked round, hoping that one among them would respond.

'As I thought,' said The Grand High Witch. 'No-one else has that power so my decision stands.' She waved The Snake Wand at the audience. 'You forget that your power is impaired. I could eliminate any one of you in an instant.'

The subdued witches returned to their places, but the silence didn't last. Before the last one was seated, a single voice rose above the others.

'It's still not enough.'

The Grand High Witch turned angrily. 'Who dares to challenge me?'

The eleven members of The Grand High Council rose to their feet and one of them answered. 'We do not challenge your decision. We agree that Ammonia B Clickfinger is too valuable to be eliminated. We simply ask that you review the punishment. Everyone here has suffered as a result of her spell and she has insulted you. She must be made to realise the seriousness of her actions.'

All the witches rose to their feet and cheered. It appeared that every single one of them wanted Ammonia to suffer.

'Very well,' said The Grand High Witch. 'I will agree to an additional punishment. All her spells will be undone. She will have to start from scratch to prove her worth. When she has done so, she will be allowed to return to The Association.'

'It's still not enough,' shouted one of the witches from the audience.

Ammonia leapt to her feet. Her face turned purple with rage. She stamped her foot and pointed at the witch who had spoken.

'Put your finger down,' ordered The Grand High Witch, 'or have you forgotten that it is burnt to a cinder. Without it you are worse than useless.'

'I'm not useless,' screamed Ammonia. 'I'll show you what I can do. I'm better than all the rest of you put together. I'll re-work my spell when I get back to Gylen.' She clapped her hand over her mouth, horrified that she had revealed the secret of her hiding place.

'Careful,' warned The Grand High Witch. 'Do not boast of the impossible.'

Ammonia ignored the warning. Her words came out faster and louder than ever. 'I'll show you who can eliminate who. I'll eliminate her and...and,' completely losing control, she pointed at The Grand High Witch and shrieked, 'and one day I'll eliminate you.'

Shocked silence filled the hall. The witches leaned forward, mouths open, watching, waiting to hear how The Grand High Witch would respond.

Ammonia's face turned deathly pale. Her mouth opened and closed but no sound came out. She knew that she'd gone too far and she'd run out of words.

'In that case, Ammonia Begonia ...' The Grand High Witch began to laugh. All around her, the witches joined in.

'Begonia,' they chortled as they nudged one another.

'Begonia,' they chuckled, 'what kind of name is that for a witch. You must be joking.'

'Begonia,' they hooted, 'fancy calling a witch after a flower, whatever next?'

Ammonia's face turned red with shame. 'Curse you,' she shouted. 'Curse you all, and curse the memory of my mother who gave me the stupid name.'

The Grand High Witch managed to suppress her laughter. She raised her hand. Silence fell as she turned to Ammonia.

'In that case, Ammonia Begonia Clickfinger, you leave me no choice.'

When Ammonia heard her full name she knew that she was beaten. She fell to her knees and grovelled before The Grand High Witch. She clasped her hands together and begged for forgiveness.

'Please,' she whined. 'Please forgive me. I'll do anything. I'll share my spells. I'll tell you my secrets.'

'On your feet when you speak to me,' The Grand High Witch commanded.

Ammonia rose unsteadily. The Grand High Witch ignored her plea. She raised The Snake Wand and pointed it at Ammonia. The snake's eyes glowed red, its tongue flicked out. There was a sudden blinding flash and the television screen went blank.

Chapter 45

'Oh! No.' the children groaned in unison. They stared at the darkened screen, hoping beyond hope that The Grand High Witch had finally put an end to Ammonia.

'What a time to break down,' said Hamish. 'Now we'll never know what happened.'

James jumped up and twiddled the knobs and pressed the buttons. He switched off and switched on again, but nothing happened. Furiously he raised his fist and thumped the top of the set. The crackling resumed. The zig-zag lines returned and gradually the picture reappeared.

There was a brief shot of the stage. Ammonia's dress and cloak lay on the floor. They looked as if Ammonia had disappeared from inside them, as if her body had simply vanished and her clothes, suddenly empty, had hung in the air before drifting to the floor in a heap.

The witches were cheering and throwing their steeple hats into the air. They were hugging one another and dancing in the aisles. The Members of The Grand High Council were huddled in a corner, deep in conversation. When they returned to their chairs The Grand High Witch strode to the front of the stage and raised her hand for silence.

'Let that be a lesson to you all,' she said. 'Ammonia Begonia Clickfinger is no more. Her name will be deleted from The Annals of Malevolent Witchery.'

Emily let out a long slow breath. 'Pinch me,' she said. 'I need to know I'm not dreaming.'

'There's no need to pinch you,' said Hamish, 'It's true.' He jumped to his feet and burst into song. 'Ding Dong! The witch is dead.'

James and Peter joined in. Ben and Justin followed. They marched round the room, waving their arms and singing at the tops of their voices.

'Ding Dong! The witch is dead. Which old witch? Ammonia Witch. Ding Dong! Ammonia Witch is dead. Three cheers. Hip Hip Hurray, Hip Hip...'

The cheer died on their lips as Emily barred their way. 'Boys!' she said with a sniff and a toss of her head. 'Have you forgotten that we still have to get out of here?'

'Crumbs,' said Hamish. He looked at Merryn with a worried frown. 'But it'll be all right, won't it? Now Ammonia's dead Tobias can come back for us. He will, won't he?'

'I hope so,' said Merryn. 'But look at the clock. The hands are starting to go backwards. Remember, what The Grand High Witch said. All Ammonia's spells will be undone.'

A strange sound made them all turn to the laboratory. The tops were unscrewing themselves from the remaining bottles of Materialisation Potion. The silver liquid was rising upwards and returning to the cauldron. Plants, seeds and lumps of sulphur flew through the air and tucked themselves back into jars and packets. The hands of the clock turned faster. Everywhere was chaos. Spells were coming undone so quickly that they merged one into another. The children watched in astonishment. The severed sheep's head flew across the room and crashed through the wall. The blue and yellow potions poured back into their respective bottles. Water flowed back into the tap. Bottles emptied themselves. Potions of every imaginable colour were sucked out into the air. In a matter of minutes, almost every bottle, almost every jar and almost every packet was empty. Then the containers themselves simply disappeared.

'Crumbs,' said Hamish. 'She even made the jars and bottles by magic.'

Emily clutched Merryn's arm. 'If all the spells come undone we'll go home. I was the last to arrive. I won't be here much longer. I'm going home! I'm going to see my mum...' Her voice broke on a sob and she rubbed her eyes. 'I can't wait but I wish...I wish we could all go together. You're my best friend ever. We've got to see one another again. Write to me. I live at thirty one...'

Her hands slipped from Merryn's arm and she was gone.

'No.' Merryn wailed. 'I don't even know her full name. I can't write to her. I'll never see her again.'

'It's Emily Elizabeth Carmichael,' said James, 'but I don't know where she lives. I'm glad she's gone home, and maybe I'll be next.' He laughed and jumped up and down with glee. 'Yippee, I'm going home at last.' He clung on to Peter. 'I wish we could go together but...'

Peter had already disappeared. 'I'm glad he's gone first,' said James, 'but I hope I'll be next.'

'Hang on,' said Hamish. 'Give me your name and phone number. Maybe we can meet up some time.'

James grinned. 'I'd like that, as long as there are no witches about. I'm James Henry Watson, and you can get me on 01631...'

He said no more, for he too had disappeared. Quickly, Merryn pulled out a notebook.

'Emily Elizabeth Carmichael,' she said as she wrote the name down. She chewed the end of her pencil and added James Henry Watson.

'01631,' said Hamish as he looked over her shoulder.

Merryn looked at the other children. 'Quick,' she said, 'Give me your names.' But even as she spoke the twins vanished. A second later Lisa had gone.

'Rosie McRae.'

'Justin Williams.'

'Ben Robertson.'

'Megan MacArthur.'

Merryn scribbled the names as fast as she could but before she'd finished, they had all disappeared. Only she and Hamish remained.

'We've got to find them,' said Hamish. 'I'll look for James first.'

'And I'll search for Emily,' said Merryn. 'It'll be less hassle than fighting witches.'

'It's the first thing I'll do when we get home,' said Hamish. He stopped abruptly and looked anxiously round the door-less, window-less room. 'But Ammonia didn't bring us by magic, so we won't get sent home like the others. What if we can't get out?'

Merryn glanced at Ammonia's clock. 'Look,' she said. 'It's still going backwards. I think we'll be all right. Ammonia must have created the fortress by magic, so it'll disappear. It's just a matter of time.'

'Well, when it does,' said Hamish, 'I'm out of here before you can say Ammonia Begonia Clickfinger. But what if someone else made it?'

'Then it'll probably stay here,' said Merryn, 'so we'd better cross our fingers and hope that Tobias comes to rescue us.'

She looked into the room where the zoo had been. Every single cage had gone. The walls began to move closer together and soon the filthy, smelly room was no more.

'Well, that was a waste of time,' said Hamish. 'They'd have gone home even if we hadn't rescued them.'

'That's not the point,' said Merryn. 'We had to do it. If Ammonia hadn't been eliminated she'd have come back and they'd have been trapped for ever.'

Hamish grinned. 'You're right, and it was fun, wasn't it. All those creatures coming out of their cages, all those crazy explosions, but...' His grin faded. 'I just hope we can get out.'

'We can,' said Merryn, 'look, the walls are moving.'

Hamish pointed upwards. 'And the ceiling's cracking.'

Merryn looked up to a tiny hole. Through it she could see a single star. 'It's night,' she said as she hugged him, 'and we'll soon be home.'

The hole grew larger. More and more stars appeared. All around them, books rose into the air. Cupboards and drawers opened. Cups and plates, pans and cutlery streamed out. Everything went up and up, floating and fading into the night sky. The furniture followed and soon the only thing left in the large empty room was a leather-bound book. It lay on the floor, and although everything around it had disappeared, it remained unchanged.

'Crumbs,' said Hamish. 'It's her book of magic spells.'

'It must have belonged to her father,' said Merryn. 'I don't want to leave it here, but I don't really want it either.' Hesitantly, she picked it up and slipped it into her rucksack. I'd better give it to Tobias.'

When she looked up, they were no longer in the witch's fortress. They were in the stone-flagged room of Gylen Castle. Without wasting another moment they ran down the stone staircase, along the passageway and out into the fresh air.

Merryn's heart leapt with joy. 'We're out,' she shouted. 'We've made it. We're safe. The witch is dead. The children have all gone home. We won. We won.'

Chapter 46

'Indeed you did.' Tobias stood before them. He took Hamish and Merryn in his arms. 'I am relieved to find you safe and sound. We have struck a blow to Malevolent Witchery and we have saved The Great Wizard. Without your warning, he would have been eliminated and this would have been a day of great sorrow. Now let me tell you what happened after I left the fortress.'

'No need to bother,' said Hamish. 'We watched it on Witchvision.'

'Then you know that Ammonia is no more, but you must also know how many Malevolent Witches remain.'

Merryn nodded. 'How can we ever beat them all?'

'With a concerted effort,' said Tobias, 'and with your help. The time is ripe to seek them out and remove them one by one. This night has reduced their numbers. Those who cheated or failed Exam 500 have been eliminated, and the thirteenth chair has not been filled. The power of those who remain has been impaired and it will be a while before they regain their full strength. Despite all this, we were not as successful as we had hoped. We thought our combined magic would overthrow The Malevolent Witches for good and all. We were wrong. Their spells to eliminate The Great Wizard clashed with ours. It took the combined strength of every single wizard to save him. The Grand High Witch, our greatest enemy was unharmed. Her magic and The Snake Wand remain as powerful as ever.'

A shudder ran across Merryn's shoulders. She'd only seen The Grand High Witch on Witchvision, but that was more than enough. The Snake Wand was the scariest thing she'd ever seen. The Benevolent Wizards with all their power had failed to make an impression on it, and yet, Tobias had made it clear that she would be involved in future battles. How could she possibly help? What could she do when all she had was The Gift, the sea-bean and hag-stone necklace, the carved wooden box, Roane's shell and a single pink crystal?

Where had all the witches gone when the Festival ended? They could be anywhere, hidden away in places of their own making, scattered across the islands, spread across the mainland. They could be in disguise. They would be indistinguishable from ordinary mortals – neighbours, shopkeepers, teachers, police women – they could be anything and anywhere.

She looked at Tobias in despair. 'How will we recognise them all?'

'You will know them, whatever their form,' said Tobias. 'The Gift will tell you what they truly are. You must be vigilant and contact us whenever you detect one of them. We are relying on you.'

It all felt too much of a responsibility for Merryn. Feeling suddenly weary, she sank down on the grass.

'Please tell me I'm not the only one with The Gift. Surely there are others, there must be.'

'There may be,' said Tobias, 'but we are not aware of them. They need to find a way of contacting us, just as you did. Although you did not realize what you were doing, your drawing of a horse's head, the circle surrounding it, and your name written beneath it, came through to us as clear as any message could be. '

'I was just doodling,' said Merryn. 'I wasn't thinking what I was doing.'

'That is the secret,' said Tobias. 'It came from inside you, triggered by a deep connection with your past. If you had simply tried to contact us you would have failed.'

Merryn's thoughts flew back to the carved wooden box in Aunt Aggie's cottage on Tiree. 'It was you wasn't it? It was your voice calling my name.'

'It was indeed and I was thrilled to find someone with The Gift. But let us return to the subject of witches. They probably do live double lives, ordinary women doing ordinary jobs until they adopt the form of a witch and go about their malevolent business. In between their infrequent meetings they guard their identities, their hiding places and their spells with equal ferocity.'

'Ugh!' Hamish shuddered. 'I wish you hadn't told me that. It's even worse than I thought. I don't think I'll be able to trust anyone ever again. I'll always be wondering if that nice lady in The Post Office is really a witch.'

'Although they number hundreds,' said Tobias, 'do not let your mind dwell on the evil things in life.

Hamish shook his head in puzzlement. 'But how can I tell the difference? They don't go round with labels on their heads. Wicked people are sometimes beautiful and good people are sometimes ugly. It's impossible to know which is which.'

'What you say is true, but I can do something to help you. Let me see the crystal that Kester gave to you.'

Hamish fumbled in the pocket of his jeans and brought out his yellow crystal. Tobias folded his hands around it and blew into the small space between his thumbs. When he opened his hands its yellow light shone out into the night sky.

Hamish turned it round and round in his hand and gasped. 'It's even brighter than before. Thank you. Oh! Thank you, but how can it help?'

'Keep it with you at all times,' said Tobias,' and if evil forces come close to you, it will turn icy cold. If that happens you must tell your sister without delay so that she can contact us.'

'There's something else I'd like you to explain,' said Merryn as she looked up at Tobias. 'That night, when you took me to the castle. What really happened to the cat?'

'We removed his collar, freed him from Ammonia's magic and sent him off to the Highlands,' said Tobias. 'He is now a wild cat and probably happy for the first time in his life.'

'But,' said Merryn, 'Emily said that the cat was you, I don't understand.'

'It is quite simple,' said Tobias. 'Just as Kester's familiar is a horse, so mine is a cat. I disguised myself as Spitfire, put on his collar and took his place. When Ammonia called me into her fortress my intention was to spy on her, to discover her secrets and inform my people. Unfortunately we had underestimated the power of the collar. It blocked my channel of communication and prevented me from resuming my true form.

'That's what happened to Kester when he lost his crystal,' said Hamish.

'Exactly,' said Tobias, 'and there was worse to come. Ammonia's evil ways were transmitted through the collar and I was turned into a very bad-tempered animal. She loved torturing me, tightening the collar and making it difficult for me to breathe. One night, despite the way I'd frightened her, Emily took pity on me. She saw that I was choking and removed the collar. That enabled me to regain my power and plan our campaign.'

'Brilliant,' said Hamish, 'but fancy being a cat. What's it like? Do you have to catch rats and eat them? I think I'd rather starve.'

'I do what I must,' said Tobias with a smile.

Merryn wasn't thinking about the cat. Her thoughts were running on more serious matters. 'So if Emily hadn't taken your collar off, we would have lost,' she said.

'That is true,' said Tobias. 'We are indebted to her, and to James and his brother, Peter. Between them they enabled us to bring The Great Wizard home. We wish to reward them, but we have no way of contacting them. For that, we must rely on you.

Chapter 47

From a small silk bag Tobias slipped three crystals into Merryn's hand. 'Blue is for Emily, green for James and orange for Peter. I hope you will be able to deliver them.'

'We know their names,' said Hamish, 'and we're going to play detectives and we'll keep on looking until we find them.'

'I wish you success,' said Tobias, 'but do not be surprised if they fail to recognise you.'

He handed a large leather pouch to Merryn. 'Inside you will find hag-stones. You already know that they are charms against witchcraft, though few in your world believe it to be true. Hamish, take the one that chooses you.'

'Don't you mean the one I choose?'

'Put in your hand, let them trickle through your fingers and you will see what I mean.'

Hamish tossed the stones about inside the pouch. Merryn listened to the sound of them jingling together. She watched Hamish's face change from a look of puzzlement to one of delight. He pulled out a hag-stone – a small jagged stone with a hole right through it.

'It doesn't look much,' he said, 'but it chose me, it really did. It stuck to my hand and all the others fell away.'

'From the pouch,' said Tobias to Merryn, 'take six hag-stones to protect your home. Place one at each corner and one in front of each door. As for the rest, if you find any of the children who were captives in Ammonia's fortress, tell them to do as Hamish did and when their hag-stone has chosen them, persuade them to carry it at all times. It is unlikely that they will understand, but do your best. It will afford protection against other witches and it is the least we can do to thank them.'

Hamish pointed to the leather pouch. 'Are those extra special hag-stones? Or can we find some for ourselves?'

'Any stone with a natural hole will have power, although contact with me has increased the power of those in the pouch.'

'I'm going to see how many I can find,' said Hamish. 'It'll be more fun than collecting shells.'

'And we'll try to find the other children,' said Merryn, 'but, please, I can't wait any longer. Tell me about Kester. Where is he? Is he safe?'

Tobias put his finger to his lips. 'All in good time,' he said. 'You will see him very soon.'

Hamish punched the air with his fist. 'Yes!' he cried. 'Will he be a horse or will he be a boy? I hope he's a horse then we can have a ride.'

Merryn was silent. She hadn't thought about the form Kester would take. Kester as a horse was more comfortable than Kester as a boy. Apart from Hamish and the few boys who had been captives in Gylen Castle, she didn't know many boys. She wasn't used to them and was never quite sure what to say to them. But her head was filled with questions and for those to be answered Kester would have to be a boy, and she knew that she would have to overcome her shyness.

'He could appear as either,' said Tobias, 'but you must curb your impatience, for I am honour bound to give you words of advice.'

Merryn tried to listen to Tobias, but her mind was full of confused thoughts. She peered anxiously into the night. There was no sign of either horse or boy. Where was he? When would he come?

Gently, Tobias turned her towards him. 'I feel your anxiety but I must be heard. I know that you and Kester share a special bond. I know too, that it will always be so. It mirrors the bond that was shared by Kester's father and the first Merryn MacQueen. But remember that your worlds are far apart. Human life is short compared to that of wizards. Your great-great-great-great grandmother left the earth many moons ago and Kester's father is still very much alive. Remember too, that Kester cannot stay in your world for long and you can never visit The Land of Benevolent Wizardry. You must inevitably go your separate ways, just as the two who went before you'

A lump rose in Merryn's throat and she blinked to hold back tears that suddenly blurred her eyes. 'I just need to know that we'll never forget one another and that we'll always be friends.'

'You can be assured of those things,' said Tobias, 'but promise to think on my words.'

Before she had time to answer, there came the sound of hooves drumming on the damp earth. She turned to see Kester cantering towards her out of the darkness. She called his name and ran to meet him.

He stopped in front of her, bowed his head and pushed his soft nose into the curve of her neck. She laid her cheek against his and for a few moments they stood together in silence. Kester was the first to move. He stepped back, shook his head and looked over his shoulder. He was telling her to mount and she didn't need telling twice. As soon as she was on his back he trotted to Hamish, gave a soft whinny and invited him to mount too. Merryn held out her hand and pulled Hamish up behind her.

'Enjoy your time together,' said Tobias, 'but return well before dawn. Go now while I rest and await your return.'

Kester nodded his head and trotted away. Together they rode over much of Kerrera, but soon it was time to return to the castle. Hamish slipped from Kester's back and went inside to find Tobias. Merryn dismounted, stroked down the length of Kester's nose and put her arms round his neck. She wished that he could stay, that he could be her horse forever, that they could explore the island together.

A voice whispered in her ear. 'You know that cannot be.'

Her arms no longer circled the horse's neck. They were twined around the young wizard. A blush flamed her cheeks. She let go and stepped back.

Kester laughed. 'Do not be embarrassed,' he said. 'I know our bond is closer when I am a horse, but do not forget that he and I are one and the same.'

Merryn tried to speak but her tongue was tied and she found it impossible to meet his eyes.

'Do not be shy,' he said. 'It is good to see you and to know that you have been unharmed by this latest adventure. Once again we are in your debt and cannot thank you enough.'

Tobias laughed. 'Away with your pompous words,' he said. 'Give the girl a hug and walk her home. Hamish and I will go ahead with the bicycles and you can follow. There is nothing to fear this night for the Witch of Gylen Castle is dead.'

As they set off up the hill, Kester took Merryn's hand. At first, shyness made it difficult for her to speak. But by the time they reached the garden gate they were deep in conversation.

Tobias shook hands with Hamish and smiled down at Merryn. 'Remember my words and I believe that all will be well. We have right on our side and right must prevail.'

Merryn stifled a sob and buried her face in his chest.

Gently, he put his hands on her shoulders and turned her towards Kester. 'Say your farewells, for now we must leave.'

Kester put his arms round her and hugged her tight. One second he was there and the next he was gone. Her bottom lip trembled and tears overflowed.

'Don't cry,' said Hamish. 'We should be celebrating. The Great Wizard is saved. The Gylen Witch is dead and there's nothing to stop us from going to the castle. We can start to enjoy ourselves.' He paused and added, 'Listen. I can hear a voice. I think Kester's calling.'

Merryn wiped her eyes with the back of her hand. She tilted her head and listened. It was true. As the first rays of sun rose over the hill, she heard Kester's voice drifting on the breeze.

'Keep safe, Merryn. Keep safe until we meet again.'

THE HAGSTONE CHRONICLES

BOOK ONE – CRY AT MIDNIGHT

On their first night in Aunt Aggie's cottage on the Hebridean Isle of Tiree, Merryn and Hamish MacQueen begin an exciting but terrifying adventure.

Finding a carved box containing a necklace, Merryn discovers that she possesses The Gift. Inherited from her great-great-great-great grandmother, Merryn MacQueen, she is able to connect with magical beings, both benevolent and malevolent.

With her brother's help she embarks on a mission to save a horse called Kester. Trapped in a fencepost by a witch, Kester can be released by Merryn between midnight and sunrise. Riding through successive nights, she and Hamish are hindered by Aunt Maggie's strict rules and the witch's powerful spells.

Selkies and Fairy Folk pledge their help, but not until seemingly impossible challenges have been met. The adventure takes the children to the Ringing Stone and the beach of Traigh nan Gilean, but will Kester finally be freed and what is his true identity?

THE HAGSTONE CHRONICLES
BOOK THREE – THE SNAKE WAND
Available July 2016

Ammonia Clickfinger is dead. Mandragora Twitch and Vitriola Sniff are engaged in a battle to win The Clickfinger Locket. Merryn finds an unexpected ally in a boy called Jake. Together with the children from Gylen Castle they help the Benevolent Wizards in their fight against evil.

But Malevolent Witches are everywhere. Leading them is The Grand High Witch, owner of The Snake Wand – a living snake that can flash its red eyes, flick its forked tongue and destroy everything in its path.

In a last desperate attempt to save his people, The Great Wizard takes Merryn and Jake on a perilous journey. But Hamish is following and The Grand High Witch is on his trail.

Far away from other witches and wizards, The Great Wizard and The Grand High Witch begin a battle for survival. Merryn, Jake and Hamish witness the fight. But is there anything they can do to affect the outcome?